shooting
stars

ALLISON RUSHBY

shooting
stars

WALKER & COMPANY
NEW YORK

First published in the United States of America in February 2012
by Walker Publishing Company, Inc., a division of Bloomsbury Publishing, Inc.
www.bloomsburyteens.com

For information about permission to reproduce selections from this book, write to
Permissions, Walker BFYR, 175 Fifth Avenue, New York, New York 10010

Library of Congress Cataloging-in-Publication Data
Rushby, Allison.
Shooting stars / Allison Rushby.—1st ed.
p.   cm.
Summary: Sixteen-year-old paparazzo Jo forms an unexpected bond with teen idol
Ned Hartnett after going undercover to sneak pictures of him.
ISBN 978-0-8027-2298-0 (paperback) • ISBN 978-0-8027-2375-8 (hardcover)
[1. Paparazzi—Fiction. 2. Photography—Fiction. 3. Celebrities—Fiction. 4. Single-parent families—Fiction. 5. Brothers—Fiction. 6. Emotional problems—Fiction.
7. Racially-mixed people—Fiction.] I. Title.
PZ7.R89615Sho 2012   [Fic]—dc22   2011005224

Book design by Regina Roff
Typeset by Westchester Book Composition
Printed in the U.S.A. by Quad/Graphics, Fairfield, Pennsylvania
2 4 6 8 10 9 7 5 3 1 (paperback)
2 4 6 8 10 9 7 5 3 1 (hardcover)

All papers used by Bloomsbury Publishing, Inc., are natural, recyclable products
made from wood grown in well-managed forests. The manufacturing processes
conform to the environmental regulations of the country of origin.

shooting stars

chapter 1

I crouch behind some thick green shrubbery to do my final check. Sunglasses camera, check. Fake iPod camera, check. Real camera (I pat my backpack to make sure), check. That's it, then; I'm ready to go. With a silent it's-gonna-be-a-long-night sigh, I reach forward and push the shrubbery aside so I can peer through. The paparazzi are there, lying in wait, like vultures. They hover around the white marble entrance to the hot venue of the week, jostling and pushing each other. They are all here to get The Shot—the one that will earn them squillions of dollars, or at least five hundred if they're lucky.

I push the shrubbery farther aside so I can see them all at once. There are more than when I arrived twenty minutes ago, ten minutes after I received my tip-off. Tonight, the group includes more than five people I don't know, and considering how long I've been doing this, that's saying something. Look at them out there. The overcrowding is getting worse every week. Now that the whole world has a camera phone, everyone somehow assumes they're a paparazzo . . .

. . . like me.

Well, technically a paparazza, if you want to be all gender correct about it, but it's better not to be female in this line of work, so I stick to "zo" like everyone else, thanks very much.

My cameras stowed within easy reach, it's work time. *Let's go, Jo*, I tell myself, fingers crossed that my tipster has the reliable sources she says she does and all this will be worth it. I'd just been settling down for a rare night in with a pizza when the call came that I needed to haul my butt back out onto the star-studded streets.

I remove my hand now and let the shrubbery fall back into place, then wait for a second or two until another big black SUV pulls up in front of the steps. One, two, three people get out. Two women and a man. As each of them appears, my paparazzo gaze flicks over them and then dulls. No one, no one, no one. Three nothings. No *ka-ching* noises here.

The other paparazzi do the same. You can almost see their eyes register "$0" as they look away. The three people are stared at for a fraction of a Hollywood second and then no one is interested in them anymore. Kind of a shame when you consider how long they probably spent getting ready tonight, but you know, that's LA for you, right? These people knew that before they moved here. Or if they didn't, they would have learned the reality of this place quickly enough.

Anyway, it's not like the truly famous don't have it just as tough. In LA, it doesn't matter who you are—there'll always be that feeling that someone more famous is lurking two steps behind you, ready to steal the limelight. Kind of like your shadow.

Okay. Concentrate. This is it. When the three nonfamous people hit a certain crack in the pavement, I get into a starter's position. And then, *bang,* I'm off. As fast as my short legs will carry me, I race over until I'm right behind them. I make sure I enter the scene using their blind spots and then carefully match my pace to keep in time with their movements, staying back just the right distance. I don't want them to notice me, but I still need to look as if I'm part of their group.

The two women *clippity-clip* their stilettoed way over the paved entry, getting closer to the paparazzi. After a few more steps, the crowd starts to become denser on both sides. The newer paps and those who can't really be bothered tonight are hanging back and we pass by them first.

One of them notices me, does a double take, and opens his mouth. "Hey, isn't that Zo Jo—" he starts, before my friend Mannie moves over to give him a swift shove to the back and he swallows his words. "Zo Jo" (as in, paparazzo Jo) is the nickname Mannie coined for me, and everyone, including the media to some degree, has picked up on it. I give Mannie a quick wink and the guy an equally quick sideways glare before returning to what I'm trying to perfect here now that I've got my walk down—my surly "I don't want to be here, this sucks" expression. To add to the effect, I whip out my fake iPod camera (aka the fauxPod) and stare at it as if my game of solitaire holds the answers to all the questions in the universe.

We keep walking and the paparazzi are getting thicker now. I can hear them talking, hear my name being mentioned. But I don't look. Not now that I'm immersed in my character.

Soon enough, we're going up the steps. Two steps, three steps. The final step and then . . . the bouncer.

"Hey, you." An arm juts out rudely in front of the game I'm playing. A big, hairy arm with a tattoo that reads "Ava" on one side and "Emily" on the other. A single date from three years ago runs in a fancy script, intertwining them. "You on the list, kid?"

Uh-oh.

Things aren't exactly going as planned—I had been hoping to slip past unnoticed. Still, it's nothing I can't handle. Hey, I've done this at least fifty times before, right? Mostly successfully.

I glance up at him and, instantly, I know how to play this. There's something about this guy that just screams "family man." He's married, judging by the wedding ring on the hand that just stopped me from walking any farther. Then it comes to me—the tattoo. Ava and Emily are twins. *His* twins. I bring my hand down, pinch my thigh hard, and my eyes start to water. I crane my neck as if trying to look inside for the no ones who have just entered the party, then I move my eyes back to him again. "Where'd my mom go?" I whimper.

For a second, his expression reads confusion.

"Mommy?" I whimper a bit harder, ramping up the volume. I really need to get into this party. If Ned Hartnett is here tonight and I miss these shots . . . He's never made many appearances, but lately he's been completely MIA and the drug rumors are really flying. I need this. "Mommy? *Mommy*???!!!" I try again. I've got to get in. Got to.

"Dude," a paparazzo calls out from behind us all, making me jump. "Have some respect for Hollywood royalty. Don't you know that's the newly minted adopted daughter of one of our favorite star couples?"

Seriously, I almost laugh out loud. Now *there's* a benefit to being half-Japanese I'd never thought of. A couple of the more clueless, newer paps start taking shots of me and I pinch myself again, this time so I don't laugh. But I manage to pull myself together enough to have one last crack at it. "Mommy?" My voice is truly pathetic. Time to drive it home. "Mister, I need to go to the bathroom." I cross my legs for good measure and look the guy straight in the eye.

With this, the security guard cracks, a horrified look coming over his face. "Oh man . . . all right, kid, you'd better go in. I don't think the people running this show are puddles-on-the-marble kind of people."

The arm barrier comes up. And . . .

. . . I'm in.

Sometimes I really love this job.

Suppressing my grin at the whoops that emanate from my few friends, I ignore the evil glares that I can feel burning into my back from the others—the ones that hate me and my sneaky ways. I don't blame them, really. I can't say I'd love anyone who had such a distinct advantage over me at work, either. And that's the thing—I *do* have an advantage going here. Where being a paparazzo is concerned, I use my age and height to get the pictures no one else can get. Sure, I'm sixteen, but I can look eleven if I put my mind to it: wear kid's sandals and a baseball cap and keep my eyes glued to my fauxPod camera. Like I did tonight.

I trot into the restaurant/nightspot/lounge/place-to-be-seen. The venue is spread over three levels, and you have to hand it to the organizers—the place looks stunning. Garlands of lights twist from the ceiling down to the middle of scattered small tables, creating an intimate atmosphere (not good for me workwise, but I guess they're not trying to impress party-crashing paparazzi). Keeping my head slightly lowered and trying to act invisible, I make my way over to a dark corner, half hide behind a bronze sculpture, and get down to business.

Head still lowered, I move my eyes up to scan the faces in the crowd. Nope. No Ned Hartnett here. Not yet, anyway. I know he hasn't come in the front door, but with these guys, you could never be sure. Sometimes they'll genuinely not want to be seen (usually when they've gained some weight in between movies), and then they'll get cagey and find back and side entrances.

I spend the next fifteen seconds forming a plan that is short, to the point, and goes something like this: lie low and leave after two hours max. Lying low is important because I don't want to blow my cover. There's not really anyone here that's A-list enough to blow it for. Sure, there's the usual famous actor here and another famous actor there, but I came out tonight for the big fish, the guy everyone's talking about— Ned Hartnett. For now, I'll be patient and sit back with my line in the water. I'll give him two hours, and if he doesn't show, I'm going home to nuke my cold pizza.

Plan duly formed, I settle myself into a cross-legged position, still behind the statue, and get in some serious quality time on my real iPod (what did people do before these things, anyway, stare into tuneless space?). I'd prefer an iPad or a DSi or something, but I need to pay attention to what's going on around me, which rules out the iPad, and I also can't risk being seen with any kind of actual camera, which means there goes the DSi. If anyone guessed my fauxPod was a shell only, gutted to be equipped with a fifteen-hundred-dollar camera, I'd be thrown out of here in three seconds flat.

As the minutes tick by and Ned Hartnett remains out of frame, no one gives me a second glance, even though it's

9:47 p.m. and should be way past my bedtime, considering how old the bouncer thinks I am. But, no. No one bothers to question me. They're all so caught up in themselves that they barely even register my existence (at least two people step on me on the way to the bathroom). I know that even if they did notice me, they'd just assume someone's nanny had, oh so annoyingly, been sick, and my parents had dragged me along to the party.

By 10:32 p.m., I am getting seriously sick of waiting for Ned Hartnett. *Come on already*, I think, jiggling my legs up and down impatiently. I'm not the kind of person who's very good at sitting around for too long. I'm always on the go, always after that elusive perfect shot. I eye the buffet that is situated below me. It looks good. Really good, considering I only got through one slice of pizza before having to race out the front door. Hardly anything on the buffet has been touched, because hardly anyone in this town eats. Maybe if I just . . . No, I can't. I can't risk being noticed. Not after waiting this long. What if Ned Hartnett turned up just as I was being kicked out? Ugh. Where is he? Who shows up to a party after 10:30 p.m., anyway? Kind of rude, no?

That Ned Hartnett—I've never understood him, anyway. He's always been so reclusive and reluctant to get out there and meet his fans. What's so hard about it, really? You leave the house, you smile for the cameras, you wave at the adoring crowds. And it's not like he's reclusive because he's one of those mean teen stars, already sick of the biz at sixteen, who secretly hates the public. He's really nice when he's not holed up at home. I simply don't get the guy.

I'm starting to seriously consider leaving when something makes me stop twitching and start listening. Instinctively, I know someone's arriving, and I sit up, instantly on high alert. The noise levels rise slightly and an almost palpable energy falls over the room. The hairs on my arms stand to attention.

He's coming. He's here. I know it. I just know it.

As nonchalantly as I can with my heart racing, I get up and lean against the wall. Sunglasses camera, check. Faux-Pod, check. Real camera, check.

I'm in a good position—a few feet from the door—but there's no way I'll be able to use my real camera in this situation, so I reach into my hoodie pocket and bring out my only real choice tonight: the fauxPod. Usually I'd be taking hundreds of shots per hour on my real camera, but tonight I'll just have to restrict myself, since I have to be discreet. I slowly bring the fauxPod up closer to my face. If anyone notices me, they're just going to assume I'm searching for some track or another.

All set.

And then there he is. Ned Hartnett.

The noise levels in the room rise several decibels as everyone sees him enter. Ned Hartnett. My eyes do a quick once-over. He looks good. Fine. Healthy. Hot (cough . . . where did that come from?). So the rumors . . . maybe they're simply not true? Hey, it's happened before.

Outside, I can hear the paparazzi going crazy. "Ned, Ned!

Over here! Ned!" they call out as one. But as he takes a step inside, then another and another, slowly their voices die away. He's out of range now.

But not where I'm concerned. Because, right now, his head is turning toward me. Me and my fauxPod. *Keep turning, keep turning, keep turning*, I send messages out to him via the universe.

And he must receive them, because he keeps turning, just like I need him to.

Snap, snap, snap. I start taking shots that will probably be useless because of the poor light, but I take them anyway, hoping I won't miss a thing. And he's still turning, turning, turning . . .

Wait.

Wait a minute.

Something's wrong.

Now that Ned's face is in full view, I keep clicking, because that's what I was born to do, but all the while, my gut is telling me something's not right. Something . . . huh . . . What is it? I can't quite put my finger on it. It's Ned all right, but it's not him. He looks different. And it's not an out-of-shape thing; it's something else that stops me in my tracks. It's his expression. There's something about his eyes. About his face. I see so many stars up close every day, I'm familiar with their every glance: how they breathe, how they move, how they look at their partners (I'm an excellent breakup predictor).

The thing is, I'd taken some shots of him last year—shots

that no one else had gotten—but the Ned Hartnett here tonight, I don't know. There's something that's changed about him since I took those pictures, and it's set off my radar. The drug rumors might not be looking like they're very substantial, but there's definitely something going on with this boy. A whole bunch of thoughts flit through my head—cosmetic surgery? Nose job, maybe? Could be, though there was nothing wrong with his nose before. Not that having a perfectly fine nose has ever stopped anyone in Hollywood from getting a nose job, of course.

Someone stalks in through the door after him. Fantastic. It's his father. Matthew Hartnett is well known for being the pushiest parent-manager in the business, and his title is well deserved. A few good shots under my belt, I lower my camera as he elbows his way in and blocks my view of his son. No one is interested in shots of Matthew Hartnett.

I'm just about to shove my fauxPod back in my pocket when something that passes between father and son catches my eye. Fast as a whip, my gut tells me to bring it out again.

And that's when, only a few steps into the doorway and thirty seconds into the party he's arrived at over two hours late, Ned Hartnett does the fakest faint I've ever seen and ends up lying spread-eagled on the marble floor.

Ned Hartnett, whatever you're up to, I think I love you.

Snap, snap, snappity-snap.

chapter 2

I manage to keep shooting right up until the ambulance arrives and Ned Hartnett is loaded onto a stretcher and carried outside. I get it all—his coming to, his father fretting over him, holding his hand, and asking people to step back every five seconds (and lapping up every minute of the attention). Then there's Ned being helped up onto his feet, plus his second faint as well, which, in my opinion, is even faker than the first one.

Over the year and a half I've been a paparazzo, I've seen plenty of actual fainting by women who've starved themselves for three days to fit into a dress and then gone out and walked the red carpet, not quite making it all the way. Real fainting isn't pretty. Real fainting is stumbling, eyes rolling back, and unflattering final poses. And Ned Hartnett? Well, funny how he does fainting quite prettily. It's all very Sleeping Beauty, and, frankly, I've lived in LA too long to believe in fairy tales.

I don't bother following the stretcher outside. The hungrier paps are still out there with their real cameras that will take crystal-clear shots. My shots from inside will be grainier and darker but worth a hundred times as much as theirs, and I'm eager to get home now to see how much I'll be able to add to my online piggy bank tonight.

When my night's produced just the usual unexciting, general shots that I've taken while out and about, like of celebrities picking up their dry cleaning, I usually upload them straight onto this website called papshotsrus.com, where they sell to the highest bidder for a small cut. It's easy, quick, and low contact, which is good, because sometimes contact means people freaking out about my size and age. But tonight I won't be selling through a website, and no one will be freaking out about my size or age, either. Tonight, I know the person who passed on the tip—Melissa, a newspaper editor I work with now and again—will want these shots exclusively. It'll be an easy sale, and I won't have to share a portion of my earnings.

When the path clears, I slip outside, avoiding the other paps, and make my way around the side of the venue, where it's quiet. I stow all my gear away, unlock my bike, and am on my way home in minutes. I take a familiar route through as many back streets as I can, since it's now almost midnight. My dad might not be here this week to enforce a curfew (not that he would anyway), but the LAPD can if they feel like it. There have been a few times over the past year and a half that they've used the minors' 10:00 p.m. curfew to hustle me off when I'm being particularly annoying to one whiny star or another.

Luckily, I avoid any run-ins with the law, and within the next ten minutes I am back home at the two-bedroom apartment I share with my dad. I lock up my bike as fast as I can, fish out my fauxPod, and take the stairs two at a time. I still have my backpack on and am downloading my shots onto my laptop when I get the editor, Melissa, on her cell.

"Jo?" she says groggily, obviously already in bed. "I take it the tip paid off?"

"And then some. Ned Hartnett arrived and then fainted. Twice."

I hear her sit up in bed. "You got it?"

I check out the shots that are flipping up, one by one, onto my computer screen. "Yep. And they look goooood."

"Send them through. I'm going into the office now and we're getting this out tomorrow, even if it kills me."

I laugh. "I'm sure it won't." I know this editor well, and she is one tough nut. I'd bet several of my internal organs that these shots will be on the front page of her paper tomorrow.

"I hope so. Now, let's talk money," she says as I hear her pulling on clothes and a belt buckle being done up.

The money we decide on (after a little negotiation) is more than satisfactory, and when I'm off the phone and have sent the shots directly to Melissa, I bring up my savings spreadsheet. This is my piggy bank. And the money I'll add from tonight, plus the money that my dad will add (he matches me dollar for dollar), means I am much closer to my goal than I was this morning. In fact, I am now more than three-quarters of the way there.

My goal? It's simple, really. Photography classes that will take me across three continents in three years and hone my skills in what I really want to become—a portrait photographer. And when I say "portrait photographer," please . . . I'm talking Annie Leibovitz, portrait photographer to the famous and infamous, and *not* Kiddifoto, making babies sit in pumpkins and look oh so cute at the mall.

Don't get me wrong, being Zo Jo is great and everything. On nights like tonight, it's exciting and innovative and the chase can be a lot of fun. Plus, it's in my blood: my dad is a paparazzo from way back. Where this industry is concerned, he's royalty. He's not on the circuit as much as he used to be now that he's traveling to and from Japan all the time, trying to establish himself in the industry there and take it to new levels, but any paparazzo who's been working for more than five minutes still knows who he is. And who I am.

Dad loves being a paparazzo and he's superproud that I'm in the game alongside him. Papping is his everything and he wants it to be my everything, too. And sometimes I feel like I'm almost there—like tonight, scoring those great shots of Ned Hartnett. It's times like these that I have to mentally pinch myself to remember it's not my dream like it is my dad's. My dream is photography classes—but there's no way I'm giving up the paparazzi game right now. The money is too good and I'll need it for school.

Speaking of school, I'd gotten a call from the school counselor, Ms. Forman, this afternoon. She'd said she was checking on how the summer vacation photography workshop I'd taken had gone (just okay, nothing special), but I could tell she was really checking up to see if I'd be back at school in the fall. The thing was, I'd gone through this phase a while back where I fell asleep a little too much at my desk and my grades were starting to slip. When the school found out why this was (too many paparazzi hours—late nights and little sleep), I became an "at-risk" student and developed an unwanted close relationship with Ms. Forman. She was always quizzing me about my grades—which actually weren't too bad, since I'd managed to pull them up again—and my friends. Okay, fine. So my friends were kind of nonexistent (I went to school on a be-there-only-when-you-absolutely-have-to basis).

Anyway, however many times I told Ms. Forman I wasn't going to drop out of school (hardly—I couldn't wait to graduate and go on to study something I actually loved), she didn't seem to hear me. Thus, the checking if I'd be back in the fall, which was getting closer.

A knock on the wall makes me jump slightly. Wendy must be home. I knock back, letting her know that I'm still awake, and within a few seconds, I'm IMing my next-door neighbor and cousin. When my dad decided he'd be working more in Japan, he bought the apartment next door and gave it to Wendy rent-free in exchange for keeping an eye on me during the weeks he is away. Like approximately 95 percent of people living in West Hollywood, Wendy once wanted to be an actor. Now she's a flight attendant who works the LA-to-London route. She only covers the first-class cabin and is really pretty and really tall. In fact, her legs are probably the same height as I am. No doubt about it, she got the good genes.

Me? I got the short genes. My dad, Australian, isn't tall, and my mother, Japanese . . . sorry, boring. Who wants to talk about their parents? The point is, I ended up a genetic shrimp. On the evolutionary scale, I'm crawling back to the sludge. Still, being tiny comes in handy at times, tonight being a good example.

Wends: Hey kiddo! Just get in, too?
ZoJo: Yep. Big night. Ned Hartnett. Good shots.

Wends: Ned Hartnett? Cool. Love his music. But isn't it your night off?

ZoJo: It was. How was the flight?

Wends: Long and demanding. The usual. You off to bed?

ZoJo: Just going to stuff down my cold pizza and then go to bed.

Wends: Okay. Night-night, sweet cuz. I have three days off, so we'll catch up?

ZoJo: Definitely. Will wait for your knock.

I manage to throw down two more pieces of pizza before I slink off to bed. And it isn't until I've brushed my teeth and fallen onto the sheets, fully clothed, that I realize something.

In all the excitement, I still haven't taken off my backpack.

"Wha?" I snuffle, roll over, and fumble for my cell. It falls onto the floor, where I grab it before it stops ringing. "Hello?"

"Jo, it's Melissa. Have you seen today's edition?"

Hardly. I didn't even know it was today yet. "I'll get it in a minute," I lie.

"Don't worry about it. I'll bring you a copy. We need to meet. Urgently."

I push myself up now. "How urgently is urgently?"

"About five minutes ago."

I look down at my exhausted body. Well, at least I'm dressed, even if everything is wrinkled. "Where?"

18

"How about that diner we went to last time?" she suggests. "I'll be there in ten."

As it turns out, I'm there in twelve minutes, not ten, because I pause to put on deodorant and brush my teeth. I don't want to scare the general public.

I push open the retro diner's door to see Melissa already sitting in the booth we sat in last time, today's edition of her paper lying on the table. As I get closer, I see she's ordered. Melissa, I realize, waits for nobody.

I eye her warily as I approach. She's not my favorite editor by a long shot (or even a close-up). There's always a catch with Melissa. Like, she'll tell you she'll pay you x amount of dollars for a couple shots, then pay you a third when she only runs one. That kind of thing.

"You've got to try this cherry pie," she tells me as I sit down. "I really need to stop coming here. Why I bother going to the gym, I have no idea."

Did I mention everyone in LA is überobsessed with their weight? I figure this probably works in my favor—I'm sure it keeps ice-cream prices down or something, and I pretty much eat whatever I want.

"Okay, I'll try it." I gesture at the waitress behind the counter that I'll have one, too. It's fruit, right? And fruit is part of a healthy breakfast, so I'm told. Melissa passes me the paper and I take a look. "Nice." I nod. "I like the layout."

"You did well to get inside. I was told the security was pretty tight."

"I pretended I was twelve and had a little bathroom emergency."

Melissa cracks a small smile. "I do love your work." She lays down her fork, signaling it's time for business. "My boss was very happy with those shots of Ned Hartnett. *Very* happy."

"Well, good. And thanks for the tip."

"Not a problem," she says quickly. "In fact, we have another one. A big one. And we'd like to offer you a little job."

"A job?" My cherry pie is placed in front of me, but I don't look at it, or at the waitress, instead just shooting her a quick "thanks." A hundred percent of my attention is focused on Melissa. "What kind of a job?"

Melissa eyeballs me. "If you don't want it, it goes no further than this table, okay?"

I shrug. "Okay." But something tells me it wouldn't, anyway. If Melissa has a job on a plate for me, it's for a reason. It's about what I can offer—a small package that looks a whole lot younger than it really is. If I don't want this job, it won't be happening.

"We need someone to go to a facility. To be a client there and take some exclusive shots for us."

"Whoa"—I hold up my hands—"hang on. A facility? What are you talking about? Like a detox place? Drugs?" I'm a paparazzo, sure, but do people think I have no limits? I mean, there's slightly sneaky and then there's just plain sick. I shake my head. Hard. "Sorry, I'm not doing that. Not for any money."

Melissa holds up one hand herself. "Slow down. Maybe 'facility' is the wrong word. It's nothing like you're thinking. It's not rehab, not even close. It's more like a retreat. *Very* expensive and very well regarded. Gets good results, I hear. Shopping addictions, bad breakups, family issues . . . that sort of thing."

I'm nowhere near convinced. "This sounds pretty dirty. Even for me." I thought I'd gone about as low as I could get when I crashed an actor's thirteen-year-old daughter's birthday party. Sure, the family deserved it, considering they'd decided serving beer to minors was a good idea, but still . . . at least I'd turned down the party favors when I left. I obviously still have some moral code about me.

"Look," Melissa continues, "there's no drugs, no alcohol, nothing like that."

"Mmmm."

"You have my word."

I almost laugh. Melissa's word? There's only one kind of "word" that applies to Melissa and that would be unscrupulous, crafty, mercenary, ruthless, scheming, two-timing, lowdown, shifty, conscienceless, dishonorable, shady, crooked, sly, underhanded, improper, unprincipled, deceitful, or shameless.

Oh, wait. That's eighteen words.

"Don't say no straight off the bat," Melissa tries again. "Let's just talk about it and see what we can work out. Ask me some questions. That can't hurt, can it?"

I eye her. I guess she's right. May as well hear what she has to say before turning her down. "Fine. So what's this place like if it's not rehab? Is it one of those places that's into weird stuff? Freaky soul-destroying hikes into the wilderness where you're left with only some beans and a compass?"

Melissa shakes her head. "No, nothing like that. Real counselors and group therapy, that sort of thing. It's located just outside of Boston. Very mainstream."

"Wouldn't it be a huge breach of privacy?"

"That's for us to worry about. We'll find a way around it." Melissa flips her hand dismissively.

I raise an eyebrow. I don't see how. What she's suggesting would be a *massive* invasion of privacy. They'd never be allowed to run any shots I gave them, and if they did, they'd probably be sued swiftly and expensively.

"All your flights, transfers—everything—would be paid for. And we'd be willing to top all of it off with a substantial flat fee, of course."

Always worth hearing this bit. "A flat fee of . . . ?"

"Fifty thousand dollars," Melissa deadpans.

Fifty thousand dollars? Is she serious? I try not to drool on the table when I hear the sum of money she's offering. Wow. They must *really* want these shots. A lot. And again, like last night, they must have another reliable tip here, plus some amazing hotshot lawyer they think will be able to get them out of the mess they'll be in when they run any shots they get. To be honest, it takes a whole lot of control not to get up, dance on the table, and scream, "I'll do it!" The problem is, I still don't like whatever this stinks of. Somehow I get the feeling there's more to this than Melissa is telling me.

I'm not at all worried about the stealth thing; I'm used to that. I've spent half a day in a Dumpster, hidden by a cardboard box. I've "borrowed" a tent from an electrical company and camped out on the sidewalk for a whole twenty-four hours, an orange safety jacket on my back and a hard hat on my head. I've pretended to be a replacement dog walker and effectively kidnapped a dog for several hours. But this— entering a treatment facility, rehab or otherwise, to take pictures—is simply . . . low. Lower than low.

I don't say anything for a while and instead pick up a slightly shaky fork, take a bite of pie, and think about Melissa's offer. There's no doubt about it, fifty thousand dollars is a whole lot of cash. Not to mention, if I put all of it into my savings account, Dad would then have to spring for the same amount, which would mean I'd have met my savings goal for school. A whole year and a half early.

Not that I'd quit papping or anything. I mean, I might slow down a bit in order to stop falling asleep on my desk at school, but not by much. And if I kept saving, I'd have enough money to do some traveling, too. Right now, what it would give me is choices. Like the other night: I'd been beat and had wanted to stay home, eat pizza, and chill out. I could have done that if I had this kind of money saved up.

It's so tempting. I don't want to do this dirty job of

Melissa's, but is one dirtier job any worse than the thirty-five less dirty jobs I'd have to do to make up that kind of money?

"How many days?" My eyes move up from my plate to meet Melissa's.

"However many it takes, but nine, tops. The place is pricey."

I take another bite of pie and chew it slowly before swallowing. "What's my reason for being there?"

Now it's Melissa who shrugs. "I'm sure you can come up with something," she says, before laughing slightly. "How about a few abandonment issues now that your dad's setting up in Japan?"

The look on my face wipes the smile off hers.

"Sorry," she says. "I didn't mean to sound glib."

It's her quick apology that gives me an insight into how much she wants these shots. Very. Badly. Indeed.

My brain goes into work mode then. I need the money and she needs the shots. My dad would tell me I'm really overthinking this transaction. I put my fork down hard against my plate and the unexpected noise makes Melissa jump. "I'll do it. For sixty thousand, half up front and half on delivery, plus a seven-and-a-half percent cut if you sell any of the shots elsewhere. Including foreign and online media."

Melissa pauses for a second or two before her hand shoots out to shake mine. "You cut a hard deal, Jo. Now go home and pack your things. Your flight leaves just after midnight. It's been booked and paid for."

I frown when I hear that. She's already booked my flight—she knew I would say yes. What does that say about me? But then my brain latches onto the other thing Melissa has just said: just after midnight. I'd better get cracking. I'll have to pack, let Wendy and Mannie know what I'm up to, do some research on this treatment facility, and maybe even get a little sleep. Not to mention that half-hour shower I'll need in order to scrub off the dirty feeling I have now that the deal's done. I signal for the waitress that we'll take the bill. But, like I'd thought before, Melissa doesn't believe in wasting a second. She slaps some money down on the table, enough to cover both our orders, and throws her handbag over her shoulder.

"Wait," I tell her, as I rise from the table to stand beside her, realizing I've forgotten to ask one little question.

"What's up?" Melissa frowns slightly, looking down at me from her lofty normal height, plus heels. She seems put out that I've asked her to pause for just a second in her busy, busy day. Even though what I have to ask her is kind of important.

"I was wondering—who's my target?"

Melissa's attitude suddenly changes as she realizes it's her mistake. "Ah, yes. I should probably fill you in on that."

I nod, waiting.

In front of me, one of Melissa's eyebrows darts upward. "Well, it's Ned Hartnett again. You saw him last night: maybe some of those rumors floating around about him could actually be true . . ."

chapter 3

Twice on the short bike ride home, I pull over, grab my cell, and consider calling the whole thing off. The more I think about it, the sleazier the job seems, and I know from experience Melissa can't be trusted. Ever since she saw me off at the diner door with her usual "Toodles, dahling!" (I really hate it when she says that), I've been thinking there has to be more to this job than meets the eye.

But I don't call Melissa, because something stops my fingers from doing anything more than hovering over my cell. And it's not the money that stops me. It's the other thing.

The six-foot-tall, green-eyed and dark-haired, good-looking thing.

The Ned Hartnett thing.

Okay, fine, so I'll admit it: 99.9 percent of stars make me want to puke. And the other .1 percent? Well, he makes me sort of swoon.

That's right. Me. A paparazzo. This is a huge fail. It's practically the first rule of the job: don't think you're anything like them and *never* think they could ever be interested in you. Seriously, my dad would die a little inside if he knew I'd had even a passing thought about Ned Hartnett that wasn't related to how I could get him out of his house and into my camera's line of sight.

My cell still in my hand, I weigh the pros and cons here.

Cons:

- SICK JOB
- WILL HATE MYSELF FOR TAKING IT
- WORRIED I WON'T BE ABLE TO TAKE THE SHOTS OR HAND THEM OVER AND WILL NEVER BE ASKED TO WORK FOR MELISSA AGAIN AND WON'T BE PAID

Pros:

- WILL HAVE ALL THE MONEY I NEED FOR SCHOOL
- CAN CUT BACK A BIT ON WORK, STOP FALLING ASLEEP AT SCHOOL, MAYBE EVEN CATCH A MOVIE NOW AND THEN LIKE A NORMAL TEENAGER
- I DON'T SEE HOW THEY'LL EVER BE ABLE TO USE THE PHOTOS, SO IT WON'T BE LIKE I'M TRULY EVIL
- $$$

Gulp. There's no denying that list of pros. Especially that first and last one. Silently, I slide my cell back into my pocket and keep riding.

After a few more minutes, I finally get up the courage to admit the truth to myself. Okay, so maybe I left one big reason off my list. One big con. Now, I add it to the others:

Cons:
* WILL BE BETRAYING NED HARTNETT, THE ONE AND ONLY STAR WHO'S EVER BEEN TRULY DECENT TO ME

That last con is probably the real reason I'm holding back. It's kind of ironic that Ned Hartnett is my target, considering he's the one who got me into the shooting-by-stealth thing in the first place.

I guess you could say there have been two major influences in my career as a paparazzo so far: my dad and Ned Hartnett.

Everyone assumes that my dad pushed me into being a pap, considering he's one as well, but that's not true at all. Sure, Dad had provided an early interest in cameras and how they worked, but the rest was all up to me.

I started with a pinhole camera when I was six. You make them out of any kind of small box that you paint black inside and put a tiny hole in the center of one of the ends, then you tape a flap over the hole to use at a shutter, and then you tape a piece of film or fast photographic paper inside the box. It's pretty cool—a camera made mostly from house-hold items.

Then I got my first real camera for Christmas that year and started developing. I had this thing for taking pictures of people right from the start. I just loved it, loved trying to get their personality to shine through the lens. When my blood relations got sick of me, I turned to other sources. Like the cat across the road. I remember I spent one summer taking thousands of pictures of that cat, trying to capture how it was in real life. It had quite the portfolio by the time school started again. Considering it was a Los Angeleno feline, it could probably have gotten an agent.

If I'd grown up elsewhere, I most likely would have continued along happily with my little hobby and become something like a wedding photographer. But, no. I lived in West Hollywood, with a dad who was a paparazzo. Growing up, famous people walked past our house all the time. When I was ten, my dad pointed out a famous actor who would jog past our house every morning. Because it was what my dad did, I also started taking shots of him. The guy thought it was funny.

He probably wouldn't think it was so funny now that he has an Oscar and I stand to make fifteen thousand dollars if he trips and falls. More if he splits his lip and there's blood.

My dad never suggested I start papping—I did it myself when I realized I'd need the money for school. It wasn't exactly the kind of cash I could make working at KFC. That said, Dad never had any objections, either. Not even about my age. Still, while he might be pushing the limits a bit as a parent, you have to hand it to him—he's pretty good at his job. He's so well connected he can pretty much find out where any celebrity is anywhere in the world in under an hour. He knows everyone—nail and brow techs, drivers, maître d's, personal trainers, valets, airline workers, masseuses, dog walkers. He knows which celebrities have relatives who'll talk for a hundred dollars. Or even less. He can recite about 150 celebrity car license plates off the top of his head.

So, that was my dad's influence.

And Ned's? Well, that came later. I'd only been papping a month or so when we had our little encounter. I'd been having a rough time of it, to say the least. I wasn't the youngest pap ever, but I was by far the smallest. That didn't stop some of the stars or their entourages from making my life difficult, though. During that first month I'd been pushed to the ground by a bodyguard, had my camera ripped out of my hands by a model, and been kicked by a singer's girlfriend.

Some of the other 'zos weren't any better. New ones, not even ones related to the stars of the field, weren't welcomed to the fold. There wasn't exactly a code of conduct and some people liked to play rough. Especially the full-timers; they hated the part-timers who liked to pap outside of their day jobs, even if their day job was school. I was new, I was female, and I was a kid. Let's just say no one was splitting their lunchbox Twinkie with me.

The night I came face-to-face with Ned, I was so close to packing in the papping thing, it wasn't funny. A group of the "old boys" had agreed on a little practical joke. They'd fed me a false lead that had me wasting forty-five minutes of my time outside the back door of a restaurant. Every so often one of the paps would swing past and go on about this spot, saying it was the new "in" place to dine—a restaurant that was actively being deconstructed around the diners—when, actually, it was being renovated and had only workmen inside. But I was green enough to believe them. After all, it was hardly all that out there for LA. There was a real restaurant nearby where patrons dined in complete darkness.

It was only after I finally got a peek inside the joint that I knew I'd never be stupid enough to trust them again. Trust was for people who didn't have the smarts, or the guts, to do it on their own.

By the time I'd ridden another fifteen minutes to the real hot spot of the night—a restaurant people were actually eating in—I was pooped and angry. So pooped that when I got there, panting, and a number of stars started to pile out of the restaurant, the hustling became a bit much. I should have given up and gone home at that point, but I didn't, because I was still angry. And because I was angry, I did something pretty stupid—I got right in there with the bigger, badder, older, and uglier paparazzi and found myself being pushed around. Until, eventually, one last shove from the biggest, baddest, oldest, and ugliest of them all had me landing in a bad way, cracking my elbow loudly on some concrete stairs.

And I am not exaggerating when I say it *really* hurt.

Because it *really* hurt.

In fact, it hurt so badly I was kind of temporarily winded and could only curl into a ball on the stairs and hope I didn't get kicked to death.

Which is when Ned came along.

"Hey, you. And you. Move. Now. Get out of the way!" are the words I remember him saying before I felt something warm on my back—his hand. "Are you okay?"

I think I'd just groaned. But then I'd heard someone else speaking. Telling Ned that I was one of *them*. I'd expected him to leave. But he didn't.

"You can't be serious. He's just a kid."

Oh, nice. I remember this comment ripping through my pain and, amazingly, causing a bit more. I might have had a baseball cap on and been wearing jeans and a hoodie, but I was *not* a little boy out past my bedtime. My elbow still throbbing, but my breath restored, I somehow managed to uncurl myself. "I'm fine," I said.

Big lie, but what else was I going to say?

I looked into Ned's eyes and saw him come to the realization that I was (a) female and (b) not quite as young as he thought. To his credit, however, he didn't turn and walk off at this point, but took my good arm and started to lift me up the rest of the way.

The problem was, being tall and well built, he may have underestimated how much I weighed, because I sort of went flying, bounced off his chest, and came back to a resting position on my feet just inches away from him.

I stood there, dazed for a few seconds, before I'd glanced up at him. "Um, thanks," I managed to say. I went to take a step back, stumbled, and Ned pulled me in close again, steadying me.

"Whoa," he said. "Are you really okay?"

I took a step back without falling over this time, but Ned kept a firm hold on one of my hands just to make sure. By that stage, the pain in my elbow had died down to nothing more than a gigantic throb. I started to think I had bigger problems, though, because I still felt woozy. And my heart was kerthunking inside my ribs. I wondered if there was something more serious wrong with me—like a concussion.

When he'd established I wasn't going to fall over, Ned frowned. "Where are your parents?" he asked me. I was still close and he smelled good—a combination of citrus aftershave and mint.

At least this took my mind off things, not to mention the biggest thing of all—that Ned was still holding my hand. "Where are *yours*?" I had to laugh at his question. Ned Hartnett and I were the same age. I'd read in an interview once that his birthday was only days before mine. He still looked confused, however, so I added, "We're the same age."

"No, we can't be. I'm . . . ," he trailed off before his eyes moved down to my hand. He let it go.

"Look," I told him, "you can go. You don't need to worry about me. I'll be fine. Despite appearances, I'm a big girl."

He'd frowned again and turned his back away from the other paps, towering over me and effectively wrecking any nice little pictures they might be thinking of taking. "How long have you been doing this for?"

I shrugged. "A month."

"And how many times have you almost lost an elbow?"

"Once."

"And other bodily parts?"

"Maybe more than once."

Ned Hartnett shook his head at me. "You've got to get out."

Ha! He wished! I wondered if he said that to all the paparazzi he picked up off the ground. I just shrugged again. "It's not forever. And, like I said, I can handle it."

He gave me a long look. "I don't know. It doesn't seem like it."

I started to get a little peeved at this point. "Are you finished? Can I go now?" I couldn't figure out why on earth he was even talking to me—I was a paparazzo, for crying out loud! The most attention we usually got was a rude gesture. And that was if we were lucky.

Ned paused for a second. "No."

At first, I thought I hadn't heard him right, or that I'd asked a different question than the one I'd meant to. "No?" I scowled. "You're *not* finished? What's that supposed to mean?"

He kept right on staring at me. "It means you look smart. And what you're doing is dumb."

That was the end of the line for me. "What I'm doing is dumb?"

Quite calmly, he nodded. "Yes. It's dumb."

I tried to control myself. Ned Hartnett might have been supercute, but what made him think he should be giving me career advice? I considered simply turning and running, but something held me to the spot.

"You're crazy. Look at you. You've got this distinct advantage over them and you're not even using it."

"Advantage?" Now it was me who paused. My anger started to dissipate.

Ned looked around and pulled me aside slightly, farther away from prying eyes. People were getting pretty interested in us by now and I didn't blame them—a couple of the paparazzi had even taken some shots. I tried not to notice his hand on my arm again, which took a whole lot of effort.

"I thought you were a kid, right? You could pass for one and get into places no one else could. Why you're out here with them, I have no idea. You could be in there"—he jerked a thumb in the direction of the restaurant—"and no one would look twice at you."

I stared at him, frowning. My dad had filled me in on Ned Hartnett, how he was one of the top five best-paid stars. But,

I mean, I'd already known he was huger than huge—I'd grown up with him. He was one of those child prodigy singers, the type who'd had a parent push him onto every TV show out there from the age of six. But the thing about Ned was that he could not only sing but also write, which meant his popularity kept growing. As he'd gotten older, he'd hidden away from the limelight more and more with each passing year, but his song-writing hadn't suffered for it. Not one bit. And he kept in touch with his fans through Facebook, Twitter, and his blog. But because he hardly ever left his house, there were all kinds of rumors about him—that he had some kind of skin disease; that he weighed over five hundred pounds; that he was chronically shy and could only speak to one person on the whole planet (his father); that he was addicted to this, that, and the other drug. But this guy standing in front of me was none of those things . . .

Well, except maybe plain old crazy, because he seemed to think I could walk into a restaurant and take shots of people and no one would notice because I was short.

"Um, and what do you suggest I do with this?" I held up my rather large eight-thousand-dollar camera, my anger now completely gone, replaced with bewilderment. A star giving a paparazzo tips on getting the best shots? If only my dad were here. Thinking about my dad, I remembered the many shots we'd viewed online together of Ned. He looked different in real life. Though that was to be expected—anything put out by his publicity machine would have been Photoshopped like crazy.

In front of me, Ned shrugged. "The camera's *your* problem. I'm just saying you're different, but you're not using that difference to your advantage. Not that I think there should be paparazzi at all, of course."

I rolled my eyes at this one. *Nice try, Ned.* He knew full well that without the paparazzi, the stars wouldn't be as famous and important as they are. The public are constantly duped into thinking the paparazzi are evil when in reality it's a symbiotic relationship. The stars need the paparazzi and the paparazzi need the stars. It's always amusing to see an actor, desperate for attention on the way up, supposedly "hate" all the fuss when they get there, then seek it out again with sad stunts on the way down.

And on the all-paps-are-evil subject, let's not forget the public. Because that's the thing about papping—it is completely, utterly, and totally market driven. If the public didn't want the photos, we wouldn't be taking them. The day they stop throwing their copies of *Us Weekly* into their shopping carts is the day we stop taking these so-called invasive photos.

"What on earth are you doing?" Someone barreled up behind us. Ned's dad, Matthew Hartnett.

"I guess that explains where your parents are!" I said cheekily and took off before Matthew Hartnett could lay into me like he was famous for laying into his son. Though, to be fair, I'd heard he had two sons. It's just that the other one was smart enough to live in NYC with his mother, which meant that he probably escaped the wrath of his father. At least on a daily basis.

I hadn't made any money at all that night. I'd ended up spending some of Dad's instead, having X-rays taken in the emergency room (a hairline fracture . . . no big deal). But despite the evening's injuries, that night had turned out to be more than a worthwhile investment. I soon realized Ned was right. I *was* different. And I wasn't using that difference to my advantage.

I thought about it for a bit, then made a few trips out to surveillance shops. A lot of what they were selling just wasn't going to cut it for me. An ugly watch camera, a pen camera, and a calculator camera? Yeah . . . not unless the nerds were suddenly going to make an assault on Hollywood. After I shopped around a bit more and browsed what was available on the net, I started to think laterally. Maybe I could buy a few objects that people would believe a kid would have on them, gut them, and install cameras inside? Dad fixed me up with some contacts, and over the next couple weeks, I had several devices custom-made. Then I set about doing exactly what Ned had told me to do.

At first, taking my devices out and about with me was a bit painful. There was no denying it was easier and the shots were better when I used my camera. The first couple hundred pictures I got off my fauxPod were pathetic—shots of stars' legs (not in a good way), tiles, car wheels, the sky, and so on. But as I kept going, I got better at it. Pretty soon, I ditched most of the other items and used the fauxPod almost exclusively. And I started to realize it was worth trying to hone my picture-taking skills, because I was getting into some pretty neat places. Not just restaurants, but poolside at hotels, onto golf greens, and even into spas and hairdressing salons. I drew the line at following stars to the bathroom. There was invading privacy and *invading privacy*.

As I used my fauxPod more and more over the following weeks and months, I thought about Ned a lot. I told myself it was because he'd been the start of what I'd become, but the truth was, I knew that wasn't really true. And every night that I went to work, I'd look out for him. I wondered if he'd be there. If I'd see him again.

But I didn't see him after that night, because Ned Hartnett kind of disappeared. He made that one appearance, then a few more, just enough so that all the rumors died down. And then he retreated back to his house, saying he was busy working on a new album and would "see everyone soon." Which, of course, led everyone (especially Melissa) to work themselves into a frenzy wondering just what he was up to. Was he planning to tour with this new album? The media went crazy. When in doubt, speculate.

That was just over a year ago and the new album was set to be released within the next few months. So far, there hadn't been news of a tour, but you never knew. Maybe there really would be if he was out on the town again. But what was with him going to a retreat? You just never knew with Ned Hartnett.

Back at the apartment, I park my bike and lock it up, all the while trying to convince myself that the job I'm taking on isn't as bad as it seems. After all, Ned Hartnett can hardly whine about me taking covert shots of him, considering my taking covert shots was all his idea in the first place.

Right?

Right?!?!?!

Try as I might, I just can't seem to convince myself.

The other thing I can't seem to convince myself of is that Ned isn't going to recognize me. There are a couple things in my favor—the night he'd picked me up off the ground and scolded me, it was dark. I was wearing a hoodie. I still had my braces on back then. And my hair was covered by my baseball cap. Still . . . you never know. I probably should have told Melissa. But I didn't.

I fish my cell out of my pocket again and start texting. Not Melissa, but Mannie.

> You busy? Have news. Taken on big job.
> Leaving late tonight.

And then I start packing.

chapter 4

"What's the job?" Mannie greets me at the front door, breathless, only minutes later.

"Do come in," I tell him with a laugh. "Can I offer you any refreshment? Please, make yourself at home."

"I will," he says, loping into my apartment and flopping on the couch, his long legs hanging over one end and his scruffy mop of hair over the other. Mannie is only two years older than me, but at six feet two inches, he was never going to be into the covert papping thing. He kind of stands out a bit.

It took me a long time to trust Mannie, but after months of him giving me tips when he didn't have to and making me laugh by making stupid faces from across the other side of a star's driveway or on the red carpet, I couldn't help myself.

He wore me down. Even my dad likes him, which is saying something. When Dad's home, he lets Mannie hang around and eat all our food.

"So? Who's it for?" is Mannie's first question.

"Can't say." I smirk.

"Who's the target?"

"Gee, I can't say that, either."

"Okay then, what *can* you say?"

"Sixty thousand, half up front and half on delivery, plus a seven and a half percent cut if they sell any of the shots elsewhere. Including foreign and online media."

Mannie almost hits the ceiling, which is an interesting sight. He's kind of an expend-as-low-an-amount-of-energy-as-possible sort of person. Mannie "hitting the ceiling" really means he puts in the effort to sit upright on the couch. "Are you serious? You're serious. It must be dirty. Really dirty." His mouth hangs open.

I sigh. "It is."

"Too dirty?"

I nod. "Too dirty."

"But you're still doing it? For the money?"

I perch on an arm of the couch. "Let's just say I'm doing it for school."

"Ooohhh, yeah. I forgot," Mannie says, and nods. "You'd be way closer with your savings then, right?"

"Right."

He clocks my unexcited expression. "But it's still dirty."

"Yep."

There's a pause. "Maybe you'll be able to do it cleaner than someone else?" he tries.

"I seriously doubt it."

"Oh."

"Yeah, oh."

There's another pause. "So you're considering *not* doing it?"

I think for a second. "Yes. No. I don't know." I look at the time. "It's just that I'm not sure I'm being told the whole truth. What do you think I should do?"

Mannie looks more than slightly scared that I'm asking him for advice. "Man, I don't know. I guess . . . if you do this job, it means you'd be able to cut back a bit, yeah? You told me you thought you'd have to. That's a pretty big incentive."

"I know."

Mannie checks out my expression. "But it's really dirty."

"Still really dirty, Mannie. Really, really dirty."

"Wait. You'd be safe and everything, right?"

I nod. "Perfectly safe. It's not sex or drugs or alcohol or violence dirty. Just low-down dirty, you know? Sneaky dirty."

"Yeah, I know." I don't need to tell Mannie about sneaky dirty. He's been there and done that. He's been papping a whole year longer than me.

"Anything I can do?"

I shake my head. "Nothing. But thanks for the offer."

"You're welcome."

We sit in silence for a moment or two until a knock on the door makes us both jump.

"Just me!" Wendy comes in. "I heard your voice. Hey, you should lock this, you know. What would your dad say?"

"Probably that I should be out working and not sitting here on my butt," I tell her. I stop perching and stand up.

"Very funny. So, what's going on? Hey, Mannie!"

"Guh," Mannie answers, and I give him a look. Mannie has a thing for Wendy. Let's face it, any male who's breathing has a thing for Wendy.

"I'm going away for a while. On a job," I say. "Late tonight." I cross my arms nervously and then realize it and uncross them.

Wendy's eyes fix onto me. "A job, huh?"

"Yep," I try to act nonchalant. "Up to nine days, depending on how things go. At a sanctuary. Should be nice!"

"Oh, like a wildlife sanctuary?" Wendy asks.

"Um, sure!" I nod. If you count stars as wildlife and me as a big-game hunter, I guess it could be just like a wildlife sanctuary.

Mannie snorts.

"It's not a wildlife sanctuary, is it?" Wendy looks from one of us to the other.

I sigh. "Look, it's not dangerous. I'll be fine. Dad would approve."

"That's not saying very much," Wendy huffs.

"It's fine, really. I'll give you a number to call so you can

44

check up on me." I move over to the computer and grab a Post-it, scribbling down Melissa's cell. I only change the last two digits. I pass it to Wendy.

She looks at it for a second. "Okay, and now can I have the real number?" She passes it back to me. "I know you always change the last two digits."

Busted.

I scribble the real number down this time and pass it over.

"Thanks. And this better be real."

I look her in the eye. "It is."

"Good." She comes over to give me a hug. "I don't like this. Not one bit. But I know you're smart. And I also know I can't stop you. If you need me to bail you out, you know where I am."

"Thanks, Wendy," I say. And I mean it. She really would bail me out. Even fly over to Boston to do so.

"I've really got to get packing and get some sleep," I tell them, and they both take it as their cue to leave.

"Okay. Well, I'm headed to the movies," Wendy says. "What are you up to, Mannie?"

"Guh," Mannie says.

"Uh-huh. Sounds good!" Wendy gives me a wink. She's used to the "guhs." At least it's endearing under the age of twenty. At fifty-five and in first class? Not so much, she tells me. "See you. And be *good*." She loads up the word with a whole lot of meaning.

"I *will*."

"Come on, Mannie, I'll help you down the stairs," are Wendy's last words as she leads him, silent and stunned, out of the room.

I manage to get to the airport on time, and it's only after I've checked in (and learned Melissa has booked me on a flight that also stops in Chicago—wouldn't be surprised if she'd done it on purpose) and am waiting at the gate for my plane that I start to worry again that Ned Hartnett is going to recognize me. I remind myself about the oversized clothes, braces, and baseball cap once more. I also know that he's a celebrity; he's probably met a million people in the time since he ran into me. Maybe he lectured them all?

Still, I made sure that I packed my bag accordingly. No caps, and the girliest clothes I have in my wardrobe. I don't have a lot, but I managed to dig out a couple shirts, jackets, and skirts, and even locate a pair of pearl earrings that my dad gave me for my thirteenth birthday. It's not what I'd usually wear, but a job is a job. I'm not going to look cool or be comfortable.

My cell rings. Melissa.

"Hi," I say warily.

"You're at the airport?"

"All checked in," I tell her. "I didn't realize I'd be stopping in Chicago."

Melissa doesn't skip a beat. "Ah, yes. Unfortunately that was the only flight available soon enough." I note that there's no "Sorry, Jo" before she continues. "One of the retreat's staff members will meet you at the other end. You're allowed a maximum of two numbers that you can call out to, but they need to be vetted by your parent or guardian. I've given them mine, but if you give me another number, I can add that as well. Do you have one?"

I give her Wendy's number.

"Everything okay with the brief?"

Melissa had e-mailed it to me. The brief, aka my job description, was straightforward: take as many pictures of Ned as I can get. Anything and everything. Ned in group. Ned sitting by himself. Ned and his new troubled friends. Shoot whatever there is to shoot and let them deal with the legal side of things. I felt slightly sick just thinking about it. "I still don't really understand what he's doing at this place," I say.

"Oh, you know. Getting 'a little rest.' All the stars need a little rest now and again from their oh-so-hectic party-going lives, don't they?" Melissa jokes. "And you know what Ned Hartnett is like. It's probably something about the pressure of his new album coming out. That he's overworked himself and it's all been too much. Blah-blah-blah. He's such a feeler. A sensitive soul. It's why people love him so much."

You've got to hand it to Melissa—she really *cares*. I can't say I'd want to get on her bad side. "Okay," I say. My mouth is really dry, and I can only manage the one word.

"Fantastic. The money will be in your account within forty-eight hours. I'll see you on the other side, then," Melissa replies, and then the line goes dead.

For a split second I almost think she means hell. And, considering the job I've just taken on, she may well be right.

★ ★ ★

"Josephine Foster?" A guy in jeans and a checked shirt holds up a sign with my name on it, which I'm surprised I can still read considering how little sleep I've had.

"That's me," I say, kind of shocked that Melissa used my real name. But then I realize it doesn't really matter. No one here is going to know my dad is Mike Foster, King of the Paparazzi. He's hardly on their radar. And if he's not, *I'm* certainly not. Sure, I've had a bit of media attention as the elusive, teenage Zo Jo, but I'm hardly going to be introducing myself with my nickname here, am I? And that's one bonus to going undercover most of the time—no one's ever sure what the real you looks like.

"Great! It's just you I'm picking up from this flight, so let's go. Can I take your luggage? Or your backpack?"

"No, it's fine." Instinctively, I grab onto my bags. I have a lot of expensive equipment in there. I'd been worried it would be confiscated, but Melissa had assured me it wasn't the kind of place where they need to search your belongings. The only thing they were worried about was cell phones, and they had some kind of interference system to keep them from working. At least this made me feel a bit better about the drugs and alcohol thing—she must have been telling the truth about that if there was no frisking of bags going on.

"Okay then, if you say so. I'm Brad, by the way. I'm one of the group leaders."

"Mmmm."

"You're not sure about coming to stay with us, are you, Josephine?"

No, Brad, I am not. I am not sure about coming to stay with you at all, I want to tell him. The truth is, I've already located every exit in the vicinity and am wondering which is the shortest route out of here. Instead, I shoot him a smile. "I'm sure it will be lovely. And, please, it's just Jo."

"That's the spirit, Jo!" He nods. "You'll have a great time. Really reconnect with yourself. You'll see."

I wish. Somehow I'm guessing the only thing I'll be connecting with is my evil side . . .

It takes around a half-hour drive in the minivan to get to the retreat. Brad and I spend most of the time in silence. I'm glad he simply points out landmarks, rather than quizzing me on why I'm headed to the loony bin.

I gulp when the large black electronic gates click shut behind the minivan and we start down the long driveway that must lead to the retreat itself. Or I'm hoping it does. Either we're headed for the retreat, or I've just joined a cult.

"Nervous?" Brad turns to look at me, sitting in the passenger seat.

I shake my head. "Not really," I lie, before confessing the truth. "A little."

Brad chuckles. "It's totally normal to feel nervous. But don't worry. You'll be right at home in no time."

I seriously doubt that. "I hope so," I reply, looking out the window. At least the retreat has one thing going for it—it's gorgeous. All lush and green with lots of rolling lawns and a thick, dark patch of woods off to one side.

"Here we are." Brad pulls up in front of a large, low modern-looking building, all glass and slate. "I'll just grab your bag and we'll find your room. I bet you're itching to meet your roommate."

I pause. "I have a roommate?" That's not going to make things easy workwise.

Brad nods. "I think you're with Katrina in room twenty. She's a great girl. I'm sure you'll get along."

I guess we'll have to. I try not to roll my eyes as Brad heads around the back of the van. *Thanks again, Melissa.*

I jump out and follow Brad and my bag inside the sliding glass doors of the main building. We pause for a second in the foyer, and I am instantly hit with the smell of cafeteria meets institution—mass-produced food and disinfectant. And it's quiet inside. Too quiet. All I can hear is the ducted air-conditioning breathing overhead, like a watchful dragon. I move my head from side to side. No one is in sight.

"It's Group A's meeting time," Brad picks up on what I'm thinking. "It's usually a lot noisier than this. Believe me, a *lot* noisier."

Good, I think to myself. Because it's going to have to be a whole lot noisier with a whole lot more people around for me to get away with what Melissa is asking me to pull off. "When does group finish?" I ask Brad. "What should I do until then?" Yuck. This is all feeling suspiciously like the first day at a new school.

Brad checks his watch. "There's only a few more minutes left, then it'll be time for lunch, which is in the cafeteria down the hall." He points to his right. "So there's just time for you to unpack a few things if you'd like."

"Okay."

"Let's find your room. This way . . ." He starts off again, and I follow a few steps behind him. This time we head down a long and silent hallway, passing room numbers 1 through 19 before finally stopping in front of 20.

"Well, here we are." Brad opens the door with a flourish.

I peer inside. Two desks. Two beds. Two bedside tables. Everything new and in a coordinating color—white. One of the beds, obviously taken, has a few things strewn on top, as does the bedside table next to it. "I like the color scheme," I tell Brad. "Early institution?"

Brad laughs. "You're a dry one, aren't you?"

Yes, I think. *But the less about me, the better.* "The room's nice. Thanks," I finally reply. I know I need to at least try to get along with people here.

"I'll leave you to it, then. You'll hear some music, which will signal the end of group. The dining room is right where I showed you before, but plenty of the kids will come down to their rooms first, so just grab someone if you're not sure."

"Okay."

"I'll see you soon." Brad nods and then turns and is gone.

I immediately crack open my bag and unpack my work gear while no one's around, then quickly unpack my clothes as well, squeezing them in next to the clothes that are already hanging in the sliding-door closet. Everything in there is very girly—not in a frilly pink way, but just very . . . feminine, I suppose. Supple fabrics, muted colors. In comparison, my cargos and jeans and even my jackets and skirts make it look like I'm a member of some kind of street gang. And they're *my* girly clothes. Hopefully this Katrina will be the kind of girl who likes to swap outfits. Then I'd totally have the girly thing covered.

I stow my toiletries in the bathroom. Katrina has a vast array of lotions and potions also, but I make room for my two-in-one shampoo and conditioner, hair gunk, face wash, lip gloss, and SPF 80 tinted moisturizer (papping in the middle of summer on the grimy streets of LA can be brutal on the skin).

Returning to the bedroom, I quickly muse on the setup

I've found myself in. Melissa has made sure my laptop won't be confiscated and will work okay (I'll need to download shots onto it) by telling the counselors I like to write in my journal on a computer. I'm not sure how I'm going to get Melissa's shots to her, because I won't have Internet access, but she's told me she'll be working on it, whatever that means. As far as I'm concerned, that's her problem. Hopefully, she won't find a way.

I've just found a good hiding spot for my fauxPod and am finishing double-checking the password protection on my laptop when some kind of music starts up. It sounds like it's coming over a built-in sound system and like it's meant to be soothing. And this must mean it's time for lunch, because almost immediately, I start to hear footsteps outside room 20's door. Just like I'd gulped at those gates clicking shut behind me just fifteen minutes ago, I gulp again now. This is it. No more traveling and unpacking. Now I have to go out there and get started. I glance at where I've stowed my faux-Pod and decide not to take it with me right now. I need to concentrate on scoping out the lay of the land first. After all, Ned may not even be here yet for all I know.

Okay, so . . . deep breath. I shut my laptop, stand up, smooth my cargo pants and T-shirt, and head for the door.

Eyes closed, I wrench it open, step out into the corridor and . . .

Bam!

I run straight into something. Or someone.

Someone's chest, to be more exact.

I open my eyes with a jolt and look up and then up again until I meet a pair of familiar green ones staring into my own.

"Sorry," Ned Hartnett says. "Didn't see you there."

So, it's not just something, or someone, after all.

"Oh," is all I can get out of my mouth as I stare at him, transfixed. Not by Ned himself, but by the light. Because as we stand there, in the gloomy corridor, a cloud must pass by and, suddenly, light enters the building and showers down upon Ned. I realize he's standing under a skylight. The effect is magical. Almost like he has a halo.

It's something else.

And the weird thing is, in that moment, I forget all about those other shots Melissa wants. If I had my real camera with me right now, I'd give up that sixty thousand dollars for one chance to take a portrait of Ned under that skylight.

chapter 5

"Lunch," I say, still standing in the corridor and staring into Ned's eyes. Obviously, I've forgotten how to form complete sentences.

"You're new, right?" Ned takes a small step back, giving himself some personal space.

I nod, very happy to see that he doesn't seem to remember me at all.

"That's your room?" Ned nods at the door behind me.

I nod again. "Twenty," I say.

"So you're rooming with . . . ?"

I pause for a second, my brain desperately searching for her name. "Um, Katrina. I think." Wow. Four words. Does that count as a record? Wait, does "um" count as a word?

"Oh, great. She's really nice. I was talking to her a minute ago—she's already gone to lunch. You headed that way?"

With great conversational skill, I nod again, my eyes still fixed on Ned. Gorgeous, gorgeous Ned.

"Come on then, I'll show you where the cafeteria is." He starts up the hallway, half turning after a few steps. "I'm, um, Ned, by the way."

"I know," I say, trying to remember how to walk and also trying to squelch the urge to blurt out something totally lame like, "I love your music!" What is wrong with me?

"Sorry?"

Wait, I didn't just say that out loud, did I? No, it's okay, he's asking about my name. "Um, Jo," I say. "My name's Jo." I give him a lame half wave and an undoubtedly goofy grin.

"Nice to meet you, Jo. We've gotta hurry up already, before all the bacon bits go. There's always a shortage on bacon bits at the salad bar."

"So, where you from, Jo?" Ned asks me as we keep walking. That is, he walks and I have to half jog along the corridor in order to keep up with his long legs.

"Um, LA," I say, after pausing for a microsecond to consider lying. But I'd thought about it on the plane—the fewer lies the better. I expect Ned to then say that he lives in LA, too, but he doesn't, which is funny because I could tell him his address if I wanted to. Which he probably wouldn't think was very funny at all.

"LA, right," is all he says by way of reply. "The cafeteria's just down here." He rounds a corner to the left, and we're faced with some large glass double doors, one of which Ned pushes open.

As we enter, I scan the large room, taking in the long salad bar placed before a huge wall of glass that showcases the rolling hills outside. There are round tables scattered throughout the room, some reasonably full, others with only a couple people sitting at them.

"There's Katrina. Want to meet her?" Ned spots a thin dark-haired girl sitting at a table in the middle of the room and gives her a wave. Katrina waves back.

"Sure. I guess." I gulp then, realizing this is it. That I'm here to work, Ned's here to . . . retreat, and there's no more weaseling my way out of it. I'm in the thick of it. Time to get moving and then get out before my cover's blown.

"Are you coming?" Ned is already halfway over to Katrina's table. He turns to beckon me onward.

"Sorry," I say as I hurry over. "Just thinking about something."

Ned nods. "That happens a lot here. Hey, Katrina," he says as we reach her table. "Look who I found . . ."

Katrina glances at me, looking slightly puzzled.

"Your roommate," Ned adds.

"Really?" Katrina stands up now, which seems to take forever, because there's no doubt about it: there is quite a lot of Katrina.

"Do you think they made us roomies as some kind of joke?" I shake my head when I finally take all of her in. Seriously, she has to be over six feet tall, easily.

"Well . . . ," Ned starts nervously, giving me a strange look.

"It's okay, Ned," Katrina says, and waves a hand. "I'm sure she's come to grips with the fact that she's short, just as I'm coming to grips with the fact that I'm . . . a baby giraffe. Wait, make that a teenage giraffe."

"Oh . . ." I look from Katrina to Ned and back again. Katrina must be here because of some kind of body issue. "Sorry," I say, "I didn't mean to—"

"Please," she sits back down again. "It's fine. How's the weather up there? Which basketball team do you play for? Guess you don't need to stand on your toes like the other dancers! There you go, it's all out of the way." She laughs now. "See? We're all good."

"Right," I say. I think she's joking.

"Ned, go and get something to eat. You're making me nervous standing there and twitching like that."

"Okay," Ned tells her, and heads for the salad bar.

Katrina lets out a quick laugh again as Ned scurries away, and I finally see that she really was joking. She pulls out the chair beside her and her wide-set blue eyes move to mine. Her hand shoots out. "Now, I don't think we've properly met. Hi, I'm Katrina and I'm tall. And you're?"

"Jo," I say with a nervous smile. "And I'm short." I take the seat she's offering. I think I'm going to like straightforward Katrina, and I hope that's not going to turn out to be a problem.

"This isn't bad." I poke my fork at my loaded salad bowl, complete with bacon bits (Ned had served me a scoop, and I'd barely been able to croak out a "thanks"). I'd made my way back to Katrina's table and had been chatting with her, acutely aware of Ned following me, when someone else had waved him over to another table and he'd wound up sitting there instead.

Well, *phew*. For now, that is. As far as I'm concerned, the less contact I have with him the better.

On a, um, professional level, that is.

Oh, man. Pull yourself together, Jo. I almost want to slap myself into line. Yes, the boy is good-looking. Yes, the boy is charming. But you are here to work. Remember Melissa. Remember your paycheck. Remember school!

"Sorry?" Katrina leans forward now. "Did you say something?"

Also remember: no more muttering to yourself like a crazy person.

I shake my head slightly. "I was just sort of wondering why everyone's here." I glance around the room. "Am I allowed to ask that?"

Katrina takes a swig from her water bottle. "Of course! It'll all come out in group, anyway."

Oh yes. Group.

"I'm not sure what Brad told you," she continues, "but we have our individual sessions with our assigned counselors and we also have group."

"Where, I'm guessing, I get to talk about my problems in front of everyone?"

She takes another swig. "You sure do."

"Sounds peachy."

"That's what I thought at first, too. But you'll get used to it. Unless your problem is something hideously embarrassing. Compulsive public nudity, maybe? Hey, the lawn would be perfect for streaking! You've come to the right place!"

I abandon my fork and wipe my hands. "Nothing like that. No streaking here. Anyway, it's too cold at night in Boston. I'm a California girl. Where are you from?"

"Chicago. New York. I'm not sure anymore."

"You're not sure?" I don't understand Katrina's meaning.

As she gives me a long look, I shove another forkful of gourmet salad into my mouth. Mmm. I could get used to this. Way classier than our school cafeteria, where the sloppy joe still reigned supreme.

"You look half-starved." Katrina shakes her head, going off on a tangent. "Don't they feed you at home?"

I almost choke. "Not like this. Anyway, you were saying?"

"Oh, right. The thing is, my parents live in Chicago, but I was at school, ballet school, in New York. But now . . . well, I'm not sure where I live."

"You don't like ballet anymore?"

Katrina waves a hand elegantly in a long move that spans from her head to her toes. "I think the real problem is that ballet doesn't like *me* anymore."

When we've both finished lunch, Katrina checks her watch. "One o'clock. We've got another half hour or so. Have you had a look around yet?"

I shake my head.

"Come on." She twists her water bottle closed and scrapes her chair back, standing up. "We've just got time for a quick tour before the afternoon session."

I push my chair back as well, half wanting to know what the afternoon session is all about and half not wanting to know. Is that group? Or something else? In the end, I decide not to ask. It's going to happen either way.

We ditch our trays when we leave, and I follow Katrina as she breezes through the wide glass doors, then across an expanse of wooden floor. She pauses at a bulletin board, where she runs her finger down a timetable, nods, then continues on her way, exiting through some even larger sliding glass doors. Soon enough, we're outside. I'm relieved. I'm not used to being cooped up indoors for too long.

I take a deep breath of the clean, smog-free air and look around me. Trees, more trees, grass, more grass, and a whole lot of blue sky now that the clouds seem to be passing. It's nice. And I'm sure if I had a whole lot of problems, this would be a great place to work them all out. *Not that I'm problem-free*, I think as I take a quick look around for Ned, who's nowhere in sight.

Crunch, crunch, crunch. I wake up from my daydream to hear the sound of gravel. "Coming?" Katrina waves from where she's started out ahead of me. I nod, take a deep breath of the pine-filled air, and jog to catch up.

We walk alongside the long glass front of the building and I try to peer inside. There seem to be a number of very similar rooms one after the other without a whole lot in them other than beanbags, chairs, and whiteboards.

"Okay, so these are all the group rooms. You'll have a session in there once every day, as well as your individual session with your counselor."

I nod. Brad had told me this on the way here from the airport. I still have no idea what my big issue is going to be, but I figure I'll just make it up as I go along.

"These are the counselors' offices," Katrina continues as we walk past some smaller rooms. "And just down there is the pool."

I take a few more steps and go over to peer in through one of the large windows. "Wow! It's huge."

"A couple people swim laps every day. Do you like swimming?"

I nod. "I love to swim laps." That was the one thing I actually liked about school—the pool. You can't think about anything much while you're swimming laps. And you can't take photos of anyone, either.

"Ned swims every day," Katrina says. "You should let him know you're interested."

I glance at her quickly. "Um, yeah. Okay. Maybe I will." I lean into the window again and pretend to be veeeeery interested in the pool. Water! Black lines! Concrete! Seriously, it's as if I've never seen a pool before. But there's only so long you can pretend to be interested in a pool, and when I finally step back again, Katrina is giving me a look.

"You're not starstruck, are you?"

Breathe, breathe, breathe. In and out, in and out. "Starstruck?" I squeak, and then cough. "What do you mean?" I manage to say in a more normal voice.

"What do I mean? With Ned, of course."

I wave a hand. "Don't be ridiculous. I'm from LA, remember? There are stars on every corner there." I neglect to mention that I hunt them down to every one of those corners.

Katrina gives me a shrewd look, her long arms crossed. "Well, good. Because there are already plenty of people who are weird about Ned being here. It would be weird if you went . . . weird about it, too."

I nod slowly. "That sounds like a whole lot of weird."

"It is. And Ned's a good guy. I don't think he needs any more weird right now. He has enough as it is."

"Right." Guilt, guilt, guilt. Because I'm not here to cause him any trouble, oh no, not me.

"I guess we should head back," Katrina says, and turns on her heel. "You're in my group—B. Same as Ned."

I'm in Ned's group, huh? I think of Melissa for a second. How . . . not very weird at all.

Katrina takes a few steps before she stops. "Just down there is the lake." She points. "There're a few kayaks and canoes and things. Some benches. It's a nice place to sit and think. I . . . go there sometimes." She glances down at me slightly nervously when she says this.

I pause for a second, not wanting to pry (me! who knew?), but something tells me she wouldn't have said anything at all about "thinking" if she wasn't open to being asked. "So you can't . . . do ballet . . . be a ballerina . . . anymore? Sorry, I don't know the right terms."

Katrina bites her lip and glances toward the lake again. "No one's actually said that. It's more a combination of me knowing my body isn't ideal, my body and brain not communicating anymore, and generally losing interest. It used to be so easy. And now it's so hard . . . I just think I might not want it enough to fight the battles I'd have to fight." She turns back to me. "Does that make any sense?"

I nod. "Sure."

"And that's why I'm here, I guess. To come to grips with that. To realize my life isn't going to turn out exactly as I'd planned it. To think about what comes next."

"You sound like you're taking it all pretty well."

Katrina laughs. "Don't worry, I'm not. It's just that I've been here a week. I've already had my share of tears, tantrums, and why-me's. And it's not like I'm alone. There are plenty of failed ballerinas out there. Ballet is cruel like that."

Huh. I didn't know that. But there you go. To me, it looks like nothing more than a whole lot of painful prancing around on your toes. "So what do these ex-ballerinas tend to do?"

"All kinds of things," she says, shrugging slightly. "Some of them stop completely, some do things like run ballet schools. I know one who was injured and now teaches yoga."

"Is that what you want to do? Something like teaching yoga?"

Katrina shakes her head. "I don't know. There is one thing I've been considering . . ."

"What's that?"

"Well, I've always really loved Pilates. I'm thinking maybe something with Pilates might be a good option for me."

"That's where they use that rack, right?" I'd taken a few shots of a star once at a glass-fronted Pilates studio. It all looked pretty painful to me.

Katrina throws her head back toward the blue sky and laughs. "You make it sound like torture."

Hey, if the shoe fits, I think, remembering that device stretching out the poor star till it looked like her thin limbs might just snap.

"I think I'd like that. Learning more about Pilates. Maybe even becoming an instructor, or opening my own studio," Katrina says. "It's something to consider, anyway."

There's a pause then, in which I start to worry that she's going to ask me about my own (nonexistent) problems, but she doesn't. Instead, she checks her watch again. "Oh, we'd really better go. I think Brad hinted that we might be going out somewhere this afternoon."

"Out?" I frown and Katrina laughs.

"Yes, out. Sometimes they let us out from behind the bars, you know. I think we're off to some kind of workshop or something. Anyway, better head back to the foyer and find out. That's where we meet in the afternoons, after lunch. In the foyer."

I actively decide not to think about how exhausted my body is feeling. After all, I'm used to exhaustion—it's my everyday operating system.

"Come on," Katrina says with a wave and, with that, we're off.

chapter 6

"That should be everyone," Brad says as he finishes counting off Group B, which seems to consist of twelve people, including me. Everyone stares at him expectantly when he's done talking, except for the kid who's hidden under his hooded jacket and the other kid who has his back to the group and obviously doesn't want to be here. Okay. At least we know the score.

"So, today we'll be going out for a couple of hours to a workshop," Brad continues. His eyes swiftly move over the group until stopping to rest on someone—Ned. "I just want to say that this has been carefully organized. The location is very private and the instructors handpicked. It will all be discreet and well handled. At no point will there be any interaction with"—Brad pauses, looking for the right word—"outsiders." By now, everyone is staring at Ned, and it's more than slightly obvious that this is all being said for his benefit. After all, no one could care less that the rest of us are here.

"Thanks, Brad." Ned practically groans the words.

"Okay, then. We've got ten minutes before the bus leaves, and I need you all to go and get changed into something stretchy. Something you can really move in. Sweats, leggings, a T-shirt . . . you get my drift. See you back here in ten."

Katrina gives me a look. "I can't believe I forgot to pack a tutu."

I laugh. "Don't worry, you can borrow one of mine."

It doesn't take Katrina and me long to throw on sweats-and-tees-type wear, though Katrina ends up looking supercool in black three-quarter leggings, gray shorts, and a Karen Walker tee, her hair up in a tight topknot, while I end up looking . . . more like I've just crawled out of a Dumpster.

Still, what do I care? I'm not here to impress. There have been plenty of times I *have* just crawled out of a Dumpster and I haven't cared how I look. Also, as Brad pointed out, no one's going to be taking any shots. Well, except for me, of course.

"Ready?" Katrina calls out from the bathroom, where she's touching up her lip gloss.

"Um, yeah . . ." I look wildly around me, trying to decide which piece, or pieces, of equipment to take. I decide it's going to have to be the fauxPod—it's the only option for a workshop-style situation. And I don't even know how I'm going to get away with that much. As cover, I grab my back-pack, empty it out, and shove a hoodie, my fauxPod, and a bottle of water in there. Katrina comes out of the bathroom and checks out the baggage situation.

"You're taking a backpack?"

I shrug. "Hoodie, water . . . Be prepared, I say." Prepared to work, that is. And because I don't want to think too hard about what I'm going to do over the next few hours, I change the subject. "Let's go."

"Jo? Jo! JO!!!" With the final "Jo" I get a dig in the ribs cour-tesy of Katrina's elbow.

"Huh?" I'd been busy staring at the back of Ned's head, watching him laughing and talking to some other guy from Group B. Katrina had filled me in on a couple of the other people's backstories already, but not this guy, who Ned seems to be getting along with pretty well. "Sorry, did you ask me something?"

Katrina rolls her eyes. "Only about three times. I was just wondering what sort of workshop you think it might be."

I shake my head. "No idea. I just got here today, so your guess will be better than mine." I give her a look. "It's not going to be some torturous boot-camp thing, or something equally stupid, is it?"

Katrina makes a face. "I hope not. I've only done one other workshop since I've been here and it was great. It was this Italian cooking challenge. All the groups did it. We had to make pasta and pizza from scratch. It was heaps of fun."

Hmmm. A couple of shots of Ned with flour on his nose wouldn't go astray. I take a sly look at him again. "So who's Ned sitting with?" I ask Katrina. "You haven't told me about him yet."

Katrina takes a quick look. "Oh, that's Seth. Car accident. He and his parents were fine, but his brother died."

"Oh," I say. Everyone's story has been condensed like this, into just a few short phrases. "Hannah, lost her mother to breast cancer, not coping well. Jamie, thrown out of three high schools, rebelling against strict stepfather. Tori, parents trying to get her to break contact with older boyfriend and concentrate on school." It makes me wonder what they'll say about me. Maybe, "Jo, no specific issue, general head case, face always glued to her iPod."

"Yeah, oh," Katrina seconds, and we both stare at the back of Seth's head for a moment or two. "Puts a lot into perspective, doesn't it?" Katrina eventually says. "Especially if you're just a whiny ballerina."

I give her a look. "You're not a whiny ballerina."

"Okay, a whiny ex-ballerina," she says, which makes us both laugh. Then we fall silent as the minibus turns right and pulls sharply into a driveway.

"What did that sign say?" I ask Katrina, jumping around to try and catch a glimpse as we pass by.

In the window seat, she twists her long neck back to see if she can read it. "Something something gymnasium."

"Oh, great," I moan. "We're going to be climbing ropes and vaulting over . . . whatever it is you vault over."

"What *do* you vault over?" Katrina asks.

I moan again. "Who cares?" I can vault and somersault with the best of them to get a great shot, but in a gym? What's the point? Just to say you can do it?

The minibus pulls up at the front door of the gym, and as we exit I'm pleased to see at least half the people leaving the bus obviously have the same feeling about this as I do—especially Jamie, the three-school dropout, who still has his hood up, shading his entire face. Looks like he feels the same way about the gym as he seems to feel about . . . well, about his entire life, really. (I'm guessing the hiding-in-the-hoodie thing has been going on for a while now.)

Brad herds us quickly inside the gym, and as three instructors walk up to us, it only takes me a second or two to work out exactly what's going on here.

Maybe it's the ribbons hanging from the ceiling, or the plates and sticks on the floor, or the trapeze.

Or maybe it's because all three instructors are wearing red noses.

"Welcome to your circus skills workshop, everyone!" one

of the instructors says a tad too cheerily and takes off his red nose with a laugh. "I'm Trent and this is Hope and Laura, and we'll be leading you today. You'll be split up into three groups and learning a variety of skills, both individual and in teams . . ." I tune out around this point and my brain clicks over into work mode, scoping out the stage I've been given and how I'm going to get the shots I need. It will be difficult with just the fauxPod, but at least there's half-decent lighting in here and—

"Jo!" Katrina drags me over a few steps to stand beside her. "Hello?! Dividing up time. You're in our group."

"Oh, sorry."

"Hey, again." I get a wave from one of the other group members—Ned. He's wearing gray sweatpants and a tight-ish gray T-shirt, and it's all I can do not to go over and grab one of those silky ribbons, tie him up in a big bow, and take some shots.

Yikes. Sometimes I scare even myself.

"Hey," I try to say calmly.

"Have you met Seth yet?" Ned asks me, and I shake my head.

"Jo, Seth. Seth, Jo."

"Hey," Seth says flatly, waving the most disinterested wave I've ever seen, which is fine by me, of course. Now that I see him up close, I remember he was the guy with his back turned to the group in the foyer of the retreat.

"Hey." I wave back.

One of the trainers, Hope, guides the group to our first activity. "We're starting today with acrobatics, which is always tons of fun. We're going to learn how to form a pyramid and also a leaning tower."

The elusive Ned in pyramid formation. Now *that* I want a shot of.

"Okay." Hope sizes us up and reads the name tags Brad had slapped onto us in the minibus. "Jo and Seth." She looks at us both in turn. "You're the two smallest . . . ," she hesitates when Katrina grunts, "so let's get you two at the back. Katrina, Ned . . ." She pauses again, really looking at Ned now and realizing he's not just Ned, but *Ned* and then a second expression falls over her face that reads "Ah, so this is what I'm supposed to be discreet about." "You'll be at the front with me."

We all move into position, albeit some of us reluctantly.

"Now," Hope continues, "the three of us at the front will bend our knees slightly and brace ourselves while standing up. Jo and Seth, you'll start by jumping up from behind us and placing your right foot on one of our thighs and your left foot on the next person's thigh. So you'll be facing front, same as us, and you'll have one foot on two different people's thighs. Make sense? We'll hold you in place with our hands so that you don't fall, then you'll reach your hands to the ceiling in a star position. All it takes is a little trust and—"

I laugh. And I must have laughed kind of loud, because everyone stops bracing, stands up, and looks at me. I shrug. "No," I say, waving a hand. "I don't think so."

They keep looking, so I shrug again. "I don't do trust. Not like this. On a plate and everything. Trust is earned."

There's a pause. A long pause. A long pause in which Hope opens and shuts her mouth several times. Everyone keeps looking, though I'm not really sure why. Don't they know it's slightly odd to go jumping all over people you barely know and "trusting" them? As far as I'm concerned, I'd trust any of the people standing before me as far as I could throw them, and considering my size, that's no distance at all. Sure, Katrina is nice and Ned is nice and Seth seems docile enough, but that doesn't mean I *trust* them, does it?

"So, you're here on a trust issue . . ." Seth seems way more interested in me now.

"What?" I blurt out. "I'm not here on a *trust* issue, I just don't like people telling me to trust someone whose name I only found out three seconds ago and who's staring like there's something wrong with me!"

"Is there a problem?" Brad appears out of nowhere to stand beside Hope.

"Yes," Hope and Seth say.

"No," I say.

Katrina and Ned remain silent.

"Jo seems to be having a small problem with trusting the other group members . . . ," Hope starts nervously.

"I don't have a problem trusting others," I say. "I just have a problem with being told to trust people . . . like it happens instantly." I click my fingers. "Like I said, trust is earned."

"That's very true." Brad nods. "But I think you'll probably be okay if you try this, Jo. Just stop and think for a second—what's the worst that could happen?"

"She might fall two feet onto the padded mats." Seth practically guffaws and Brad shoots him an are-you-Jo? look.

"I might fall two feet onto the padded mats and crack my teeth and need painful and expensive dental work because I trusted people I don't really know that much about," I say to Seth, before turning to Brad. "Anyway, that's not the point. It's not that I think something bad is going to happen, it's that I object to meaningless trust games. I don't think anyone's going to drop me, but I don't think I'll trust them any more if they don't drop me, either."

I look around to see the other groups have stopped what they're doing and are watching me now. Ugh . . . how did we get here? From doing silly circus exercises to this? I don't want to be arguing. It's stupid, I knew it would be stupid, and I should just put up with it being stupid. *You're here to work, Jo*, I remind myself. *You've put up with way worse in your time.* So what's the problem?

"Look," I say, shaking my head, "don't worry about it. I'll do it."

"You don't have to if you don't want to," Brad says, doing his best I-understand-you-Jo face.

Double ugh. There's nothing to understand. "I said I'd do it," I tell him from between gritted teeth. "Now can we just get on with it, already?"

Ned takes a step forward and offers me his hand. "Come on, Jo. Walk all over me. You know you want to." He's trying to make light of the situation, which is sweet, but I'm still in a huff.

"Well?" I turn around to everyone else, but I take Ned's hand, which is warm and strong, just like it was that night he picked me up off those concrete steps. Before I know it, he's braced in the position Hope demonstrated before, and I've jumped on his left thigh.

"Good work, Jo," Brad says, and it takes every ounce of energy I have to ignore him. Could he be any more sharing and caring? I am so getting these shots and getting out of here. In the next five minutes, with any luck.

Hope steps in beside me and I place my left foot on her right thigh, then I look to my right at Ned, to let him know I'm about to remove my hand from his. "I won't drop you," he says, as my eyes meet his and I start to say something because I think he's being sarcastic, but when I see his expression, I realize he's not. He's not being sarcastic at all.

"Um, good," I kind of gulp and then look away, pretending to concentrate.

Within another thirty seconds, we've done it. I have one foot on Ned's thigh and another on Hope's, my arms high in the air, as does Seth.

Well, yay, team.

"Thanks, Hope. That was great," I deadpan as I jump off both her and Ned, whose gaze I avoid. And I can't wait to see whom I'll be trusting with my life next.

Naturally, Hope jumps around and claps as if we've all done something mind-blowingly spectacular, instead of clambering all over each other like puppies. "That was fantastic, guys! Great teamwork! Let's move onto the next station for today—the high wire. Not so high today for safety reasons, of course, but you'll be amazed how fast your balance will come along. It's a great one for trusting in your *own* abilities." Her eyes flick over to me.

Oh, great.

"Should work for Jo," Seth says under his breath, and I choose to ignore him, as well as Hope. *You're here to work, here to work, here to work*, I chant to myself.

Hope guides us over to the next activity and we line up, ready to take our turn. Katrina and I are at the back of the line and as we wait she touches a hand to my right shoulder. "Are you okay?" She gives me a concerned glance.

I turn around slightly to look at her, my arms crossed, and I sigh, shaking my head slightly. "I don't know; that was weird. It just all got on my nerves. I don't like people telling me what to do. I'm not used to it."

Katrina laughs. "We make a good pair, then. One of my big problems is that I *don't* have people telling me what to do every minute of the day anymore, and I'm a bit lost without it. Monday: ballet, pointe, lunch, ballet, modern dance. Tuesday: ballet, body mechanics, lunch, repertory, ballet. Wednesday: ballet, pointe, lunch, ballet, theater dance . . . You get my drift."

"That's some routine. Didn't it drive you just a little nuts being told what to do every minute of every day?"

Katrina shrugs slightly. "It was the way things were. And everyone I knew was doing the same thing as I was day after day, so it was normal, I guess. But you go to school, it must be the same for you?"

I raise an eyebrow. "I guess." I fail to mention falling asleep at my desk because of my nighttime activities.

Katrina goes to say something, but Hope calls out to me at the same time, signaling that it's my turn. I give Katrina a grin and hop up onto the high wire, which we should definitely be calling a low wire today.

And while everyone else had taken their time, I practically skip across it, just as I knew I would. My balance is excellent. It has to be if you spend half your life wedged perilously on top of spiky gates, leaning over car hoods, perched on mailboxes, and so on. Being built like a gymnast helps, too.

"Wow, Jo. That was amazing. Your balance is spot on!" Hope applauds. I nod, only half hearing what she's saying because I'm focused on Ned, who's standing in line behind Katrina. Somehow, some way, I have to get a shot of this—of Ned balancing on the wire, his arms outstretched, looking shaky. Like his life. They'll be good shots. If I can get them.

"I'm a little cold," I say to Hope, even though it's a lie. "I'm just going to throw another layer on." I point to my backpack that's resting against the opposite wall. In front of me, Hope nods absentmindedly as she watches Katrina step up to the low wire. I pause for a second, thinking that with her skills she'll nail it, then remember her mind-body disconnect and watch a bit harder.

Katrina steps onto the thick wire and is suddenly all over the place, despite her attempts to apply the tips Hope starts firing at her. She finally makes it to the other side, with all the grace of a baby hippo. "Elegance in action," she says, coming to stand beside me, once Hope has finished her "Great try, Katrina!" pep talk.

"Growing sucks," I tell her, crinkling my nose. "Not that I'd know . . . which is kind of my point. Growing or not growing. Sucks either way."

Katrina nods. "I hear you."

Ned steps up to the low wire now, and I remember what I'm supposed to be doing. "I'm freezing," I lie to Katrina as well. "I'll be back in a second." I point to my backpack again and hurry off.

Got to get this shot. Got to get this shot.

I grimace slightly as I cross the room, thinking of Ned being so nice before—offering his hand, telling me he wouldn't drop me—and then shake my head, trying to ditch the memory.

When I reach my backpack, I kneel down on the floor and open it up, rustling inside as if I'm looking for my hoodie. Instead, I fiddle with my fauxPod, thinking about how I'm going to do this. It won't be easy. Maybe if I . . . okay. That might work. I stand up and slide my left arm and my head into my hoodie, so if anyone looks, it seems as if I really am busy putting on that extra layer. As I'm rummaging around, my stomach gives an unhappy squeeze. Obviously it doesn't want to be a part of this, and I can't really say I blame it.

I poke the very end of the fauxPod, where the camera is hidden, out of my right sleeve, aim, and guess like I've never guessed before. No wonder Melissa is paying me the big bucks for this job—there's no way someone would be able to get these shots without having had a lot of on-the-job faux-Pod training.

When I think I might actually have something, I bend over to my backpack again and take a quick scroll through. Terrible, terrible, not too bad, okay, terrible, good, pretty good, and that's the one—that's it, my first decent shot to send to Melissa. I click the fauxPod closed, zip up my back-pack, and head over to the group.

And as I join them again, Ned meets my eyes and smiles, and my stomach does that squeezing thing once more, same as it did when I'd taken that one decent shot. Well, decent for me, but not so decent for Ned. Because those first shots of Ned? They're not exactly flattering, and I'm guessing any other shots I take today won't be, either. I know the angle Melissa will go for on them, too—it'll be all "star's life hangs in the *balance.*"

Another squeeze from my stomach. And I don't think it's the bacon bits giving me grief.

I think it might be my conscience.

chapter 7

Over the next few hours, we take a crack at juggling, spinning plates on sticks, tumbling, and trapezing. By making
fake trips for a drink of water and a tissue, I manage to get
another two decent shots of Ned. And the more I take, the
less painful it becomes. He's not Ned. He's a target. A target
to point my camera at and shoot. I need to remember that.

Just after 4:00 p.m., Brad rounds us up and we head
back to the minibus. Busy messing around with my backpack, I'm one of the last on the bus. With Brad already sitting beside Katrina, there's only one seat left—right at the
front with Seth.

Fantastic.

I thump down next to Seth, who gives me a fake

so-happy-to-see-you! grin and then goes back to the book he's reading. Feeling a bit cold, I pick up my backpack from where I've kicked it under the seat and open it up, rustling around inside for my hoodie, which I'd taken off again after our low wire fun.

"Hey! I wasn't allowed to keep my iPod . . . ," Seth says, making a grab for my fauxPod. I immediately panic and overreact, snatching it back out of his hand with full force. "Leave it," I tell him.

Seth gives me a weird look. "You really do have issues."

"Only with you," I tell him, concentrating on zipping up my backpack and shoving it under the seat again.

Behind us, someone leans forward and taps Seth on the shoulder. "Mind if we switch?" Ned asks.

"More than fine with me," Seth says, and stands up on the seat. He jumps over me, and I shuffle sideways so I'm sitting next to the window. "Good luck, man, you'll need it," Seth tells Ned as he sits down next to me, the seat's padding making a whooshing noise as he does.

"Looks like you're stuck with me now!" Ned grins, not looking at all displeased.

"Yup," I say, glancing at him for a split second only.

"Are you always this grumpy?"

I don't look at him. "Yup."

He laughs. "I liked your stance on trust. I mean, who really trusts people just because they've shared some odd clowning experience?"

"Exactly my point!" I throw one hand in the air and turn back, suddenly feeling animated. "It's just so fake. I really don't see the point." I swivel around to face Ned now, who nods in agreement, encouraging me. "I stand on you and you don't drop me and suddenly you're trustworthy? I seriously doubt it."

"Good to know how you feel." Ned laughs again. "Also good to know you're not always grumpy."

I twist my mouth, then can't help but laugh. "I'm usually pretty close to grumpy, so watch out."

"Oh, I will."

There's a pause in which I realize I need to acknowledge the big F. Fame. "So, you're famous, huh? Singing, songwriting. The whole deal. How's that treating you?" May as well cover all bases.

Ned laughs again. "Not so great, obviously. Seeing as I'm here spinning plates on sticks."

"Fame. It's not all it's cracked up to be, is it?" I shrug slightly, then realize that's going to sound more than a little random. "Er, not that I'd know. But so I hear. Was circus skills *discreet* enough for you?" My eyes swivel in Brad's direction.

Ned groans just like he did earlier. "He may as well have put a flashing sign over my head. Up until this point I'd thought I was doing a good job of lying low."

I almost laugh. Ned is kidding himself if he thinks he's lying low; his looks are just a tad too Hollywood. He'd be the kind of person who would turn heads just walking down the street even if he *weren't* Ned Hartnett, if that makes any sense. He has the X factor thing going on.

I glance at him sideways just to check that he still has it (oh yes, and then some), but then I frown slightly. Because that feeling I'd had the other night about him seeming different—I get it again. I think harder about it now, but I still can't figure out what it is. He looks exactly the same as the night of the painful elbow, but . . . no, wait. That's it! The difference I'm picking up on is from remembering this other time, about a year ago, when I'd taken some exclusive shots of him outside his house.

It had been the only time I'd taken shots of Ned, and he'd looked really different. Almost not like himself, because his face had been so twisted with pain. That was the thing— he'd been really sick (with appendicitis, as it turned out). And while he doesn't look sick at all now, for some reason I'm reminded of that night. I've never been able to forget how different he'd looked.

"So." Ned's voice fills the silence between us, drawing me back to the present. "Are you going to let us all know why *you're* here? We have several guesses so far. From running away from home to won't attend school to trust issues."

I snort. "Let me see. That last guess is Seth's?"

"Bingo," Ned answers. "I take it you wouldn't agree with him?"

"Hey, I'm not giving anything away at this point. It's only fair to let them guess a little longer. They look like they could use some excitement in their lives." I expect to see some kind of reaction from Ned when I say this, but I don't get anything. When the silence becomes unbearable, I can't help but start talking again. "Fine. To tell you the truth, I can't give you a reason why I'm here."

"You don't know why?" Ned frowns.

I shrug again, not wanting to lie outright. So far, what I've said is completely true. I can't exactly tell Ned why I'm here, can I? I can't let him know that Brad, while trying to be so careful and discreet, has actually managed to invite the enemy right on board the minibus.

"That makes two of us, then," Ned replies.

Now it's me who frowns. "You don't know why you're here?" I ask Ned.

Frustratingly, he copies my shrug. And it's only then that I note he's echoing my neutral words. I told Ned I can't give him a reason I'm here. And that's the same thing he's just told me. Quickly, I take a look at his expression to see if he's playing some sort of game, but he doesn't seem to be. Instead, he's looking out the front window now, kind of lost in thought.

I decide to let it slide.

"What happens when we get back?" I ask Ned after a while.

He turns to look at me, but only says one word . . .

"Group."

I could panic about group, but I don't. I figure panicking would be a very bad idea considering the trust babble that had come out of my mouth during my circus skills stint. Instead, I try to keep my mind on the job and think about how I can get a few shots out of this. I can't see how that's going to happen, considering group has us all sitting on chairs, facing each other in a circle.

Brad starts group by having everyone tell me their names and where they're from, gets me to give a short intro, then moves on to talk about the afternoon's workshop.

"It looked like everyone had a great time," he says. "Anyone learn anything in particular that they want to share?"

"I learned that my balance is as shot as it was a week ago!" Katrina pipes up.

"You might think so, but I saw you on that wire. You don't give up, Katrina. You're a fighter. You mastered it in the end. You really tried."

"Yeah, well. *Trying* doesn't cut it at ballet school, unfortunately."

"And how does that make you feel?" Brad leans forward.

"As over it all as I was a week ago," Katrina says, and crosses her arms.

"Anyone else feel that way?" Brad looks around the group. Everyone remains silent.

"Jamie?" Brad chooses to single out Hoodie Boy. "It was great to see you join in with the juggling activity."

Seth does his usual guffaw. "I don't think someone

86

throwing a ball and it bouncing off you really counts as 'joining in.'"

I have to force myself not to sigh out loud. If only Seth was my target, I'd feel more than fine about taking shots of him for cold hard cash all day long.

Brad ignores his comment. "Seth, it was great to see you bonding with Group B. You got right in there with the acrobatics."

"Yeah," Seth replies, probably not smart enough or fast enough to turn this around into something nasty. And I can practically read Brad's thoughts. Poor Seth. Attacking to get rid of his pain. Yeah, right. I'd bet my trigger finger Seth attacks not because of his pain, but because he's a pain in the you know what and always was.

Oops.

I must shake my head slightly or something with this thought, because Brad's attention turns to me now.

"Jo. You did well toward the end of the workshop."

"Um, thanks," I say slowly.

"But there were a few issues at the start. Did you want to talk about that?"

No, I think. But somehow I'm guessing that's not the answer Brad is looking for here. "No issues." I shrug slightly, reminding myself to keep this light. Light and nonspecific.

"You mentioned a few things about trust . . . ," Brad says, urging me on.

"Mmmm."

"Where do you think those thoughts came from?"

"Um . . ."

Brad looks down at the clipboard he's carrying. "You mentioned before that you live in LA."

"Yeeesss," I agree, wary of being trapped.

"And you live with?"

I glance around the group and see that everyone is waiting for an answer. For a split second, I think about making up some whole other life, but know I'd just trip myself up at some stage or another. Anyway, it's not like I even need to lie. They won't be able to link me to my dad or my work, so I decide to tell a version of the truth. Truth lite, I'll call it. "I live . . . with my dad."

"That's a good start." Brad nods. "And he's happy that you're here?"

I pause. Unless Wendy's told him, my dad doesn't exactly know that I'm here. "He's fine with it," I say slowly. "He's in Japan for the next week or so, anyway."

"He's in Japan?" Brad says. "For work?"

I nod, realizing I've already said more than enough for Brad to go with.

"Does he travel there often?"

I shrug. "A bit. But my cousin lives next door, so it's fine."

"And your mom?"

"I just have my dad," I say quickly, not really liking where this is going and already feeling more than slightly trapped.

"Which is fine," I add. "It's not a problem. I like it that way. He likes it that way. Everyone's happy."

"That's good." Brad nods.

"Works for us."

"Great!" Brad says. "So, if you could choose what your life would be like, completely change it overnight and wake up tomorrow, you'd choose the same setup? Everything the same?"

I take a deep breath. Oh, please. This is just like the trust bit again. He's twisting my words. "As if anyone would."

"What do you mean by that?"

"Well, everyone would change something about their lives, wouldn't they?"

Brad pauses for a beat or two. "Would they?"

"Wouldn't you?" I zing back.

"I don't think so."

"Then you're a lucky man, Brad." Man, what a liar. I can guarantee he thinks he doesn't get paid enough.

"I *am* a lucky man, but back to you, Jo. How about you? Is there something in particular you'd change?"

I've just about had enough. If he thinks I'm going to admit to a fantasy of a mom, a dad, a brother, a dog, and a white picket fence, he has another think coming. I look serious for a second. "Probably the toaster. It's way too deep and my waffles always get stuck at the bottom and I have to fish them out with a knife. Of course, I unplug it first and everything, because even though my dad works away a lot, I'm really responsible, but it's very annoying. It'd be nice to have pristine nonstabbed toaster waffles every morning. That and there's a dog across the street that barks at three a.m. that I could happily murder."

Across the room, Ned laughs slightly, then coughs. "Sorry." He moves in his seat.

Brad's attention only flickers away from me for a second. That is, until a whimpering sound starts up from Seth that makes all of us turn and look at him. Suddenly, without warning, Seth stands up, his chair falling behind him. "I'm just so angry. With myself. With my parents. With my brother. With the world." He starts to cry and sort of choke at the same time. And then the most amazing thing happens—this weird, random snot bubble accidentally emerges from his nose.

We all stare at him, openmouthed.

Brad looks around the circle. "I think we might continue our discussion tomorrow, Group." He stands up and moves over toward Seth, who is now blowing his nose and looking a bit embarrassed and confused at what just happened. "Seth, why don't you come into my office and we'll chat."

Wow. How about that. I feel bad about what happened to Seth and everything, but there's no doubt about it—the guy has good timing.

★ ★ ★

The rest of the day goes pretty smoothly. At dinner, there are a few questions here and there about my dad being away a lot. The people who ask aren't even prying, they mostly want to check out how they can set up the same kind of life-style for themselves, which is pretty funny, since it's just everyday life for me. After dinner everyone heads back to their rooms, or hangs out in the communal living room watching TV.

"Um, Jo, right?" A guy I've seen around the place, but who isn't in my group, approaches the couch I'm sitting on in the living room with Katrina.

"That's me," I say, and glance up.

"Phone message for you." He passes me a slip of paper. Before I can ask him anything else, he takes off again. I unfold the piece of paper. "Just checking in on you," it says. "Always here if you need me, Wendy."

"It's from my cousin," I turn and say to Katrina. "She watches out for me."

"She lives with you?" Katrina asks.

I shake my head. "Next door. But she's really cool. She's a flight attendant and gets to meet the most amazing people. And she cracks me up—she likes to tell people our living arrangement is all set up like *Friends* or *Melrose Place*. Just without the ugly naked guy or weird lady with the wig."

"Sounds like fun," Katrina says. "More fun than having two sisters, anyway. Those two would walk over my dead body just to get my hair straightener."

I laugh at this. "You wouldn't trade them," I tell her. The thing is, I barely know Katrina and I've already heard a lot about her sisters. The three of them are obviously pretty tight, despite living in different cities.

"Not today, anyway. Ask me again when I get back home and you might hear a different story!"

I fold the note up again. "What I don't get is why they didn't come and find me when Wendy called? I mean, I must have been right here."

"No phone calls." Katrina shakes her head. "We have family phone call night and that's it. Unless your counselor thinks a call is necessary, or whatever. It's just that a lot of the kids here can get hassled by their families for various reasons. We're supposed to be having "me" time, remember? To be honest, I really don't know how you even got a message."

"Oh, right." I do. Wendy could charm anyone into doing anything.

"Well," Katrina's eyes move back to the TV, "there's only so much *Bachelorette* I can take. I'm going back to the room. What about you, Jo?"

I glance at her as she gets up and then take another quick look in Ned's direction. He's still watching TV, too. "Maybe soon. You never know. Someone could beat someone else to death with that last rose. It might happen."

Katrina laughs as she starts off. "In your dreams."

During the commercial break, I continue to pat my

fauxPod that's been stowed in the front pocket of my hoodie since dinnertime. I'd managed to take a few shots of Ned eating, but so what? Hardly very exciting stuff. And sitting in front of the TV . . . wow. Big deal.

Thinking about him, my eyes move in Ned's direction again and collide with his. Quickly, I move them away, only to find them moving back again, uncontrollably, mere seconds later. He's still looking at me. Busted, this time we both flash guilty smiles.

We go back to watching TV after that, but something plays on my mind as I watch—that smile of Ned's. For an instant there, it seemed different again. That is, Ned seemed different. I wish I could put my finger on whatever it is that's bugging me about him lately. It's definitely something, that's for sure.

When the show ends, Ned's smile is still on my mind, and I find my gaze sliding back toward him again.

Oops.

Our eyes collide once more.

And, this time, Ned really laughs. He gets up and comes over to sit closer to me. I try to remain calm, but I think my heartbeat may be giving me away. It's practically louder than the TV.

"Sorry to stare," he says.

"You weren't staring," I tell him.

Ned doesn't reply, but stares at the TV instead, where some vividly colored cereal is dancing around in a kid's bowl, while some mother type tries to convince us it's actually healthy. Mid-vitamin-and-iron statement, he turns back, his eyes focusing in on me. "I've been thinking about it a lot this evening—what would you really change?"

I suck in my breath a tad too noisily. Ned's expression is serious and his gaze intent. He's looking for a real answer here. Not a Brad answer. "I . . . ," I start, before changing tack. "You first."

Ned bites his lip for a second, but his eyes don't move from mine. "Almost everything about my dad," he snorts slightly. "That's a given."

I get a mental picture of Matthew Hartnett. I don't blame him.

He looks away now. "And there's something I did in the past. A stupid mistake." He's silent for a moment or two, thinking, before his focus moves back to me again. "You?"

I stare into his green eyes and want to give him the answer he deserves, so I tell him the truth. "I don't think there is any one thing. There's something I'm working toward and I'll get there in the end. But it'll take a while." I'd never spoken more than a few words to the stars I shot on a daily basis until I'd met Ned. And now I wondered whether I could still do my job if I got to know them like this—as real people. I feel that tightness in my stomach repeat and refocus as I stare at a spot in the distance.

Silence.

Ned looks at the TV again, me at a worn spot on my

jeans. As we sit there, just for a moment I let myself imagine what it might be like to be normal—just a normal girl (fine, a slightly messed-up version of a normal girl) sitting here next to Ned. A girl who wasn't a paparazzo. A girl who could . . . turn around and kiss him. Just like that. Completely out of the blue. Because she so desperately wanted to.

I let myself imagine this, but just for a moment.

"Can you change your stupid mistake?" I blurt out way too fast, not even thinking about the words as they exit my mouth. They're so unexpected, they must come straight from my subconscious.

The silence that follows is almost unbearable, even with the TV droning on in the background.

He doesn't look at me. "I can't go back, but I'm trying in a different way. I hope it works." He glances at me now. "I really hope so."

Whatever it is, it looks like it hurts. And in that moment, I feel awful for Ned. He seems suddenly so . . . real. Not a target, but a living, breathing human being that feels things. Whatever he's thinking about, he's concentrating on it so hard it's almost tangible. It seems as if it's hanging between us by a thread and I know that even if I could take a shot of this moment, it's something that might not show up.

Maybe not everything can be seen through a lens.

"Hey, are you Jo Foster?" a guy's voice calls out from the corridor that leads from the office to the communal living room. Ned and I both turn to look at him. I've seen him before, working in the office area. He's youngish and is wearing one of the retreat's staff polo shirts.

I nod, and when I do, his gaze flicks over to Ned. Instantly, I know this is about work. "Sorry," I say to Ned. "I'd better see what he wants."

"Sure," Ned answers, and turns back to the TV.

I get up and go over to the guy—his name, embroidered on his T-shirt, reads "Rowan." "Yes?" I say when I reach him.

He nods with his head, indicating that we should step farther down the corridor, completely out of earshot. After we do, he glances around before he speaks. "If you need to use the, um, facilities in your room, you can do that tonight from nine to ten p.m."

Ah, right. I'd wondered how Melissa was going to arrange for me to e-mail through her shots—it looks like Rowan is going to be doing that arranging. I check my watch; it's eight thirty. When I look back up again, I inspect Rowan with a frown. I don't think he's used to this kind of thing—he's sweating. Beads of perspiration are dotted all over his top lip. Maybe he's not as familiar with the dark side as I am.

"Thanks," I tell him. "Try not to have a heart attack, okay?" And with a shake of my head, I go back to the communal living room. Ned's still there, sitting on the couch. He glances up at me when I drop back into my seat.

"The bureaucracy here," I say, and shrug, "it's never ending. I mentioned on one form that I was lactose intolerant and everyone suddenly seems to think I'm going to go into anaphylactic shock if I'm in the same room as milk." This was close to the truth—I am lactose intolerant, and every time I enter the cafeteria, one of the staff makes sure to let me know which items have dairy in them and provides me with my own soy milk. Which is really nice of them, but I'm kind of used to fending for myself when it comes to dairy. Even so, I feel bad about lying to Ned.

Yet again.

"That must suck," Ned replies. "I don't know if I could give up milkshakes."

I nod absentmindedly, not thinking about milkshakes, but thinking that it *does* suck. Lying to Ned sucks. Big-time.

Especially because I know that I'm going to have to keep on doing it.

chapter 8

I can hardly believe I have the guts, but at 9:47 p.m., during my time with the "facilities," I decide to play Melissa. I e-mail and tell her getting decent shots is harder than I thought it would be. Because I leave it till the last minute, Melissa doesn't have time to reply, and, for a while at least, I'm off the hook.

By lunchtime the following day, I've taken only a few more shots of Ned and they're all terrible. I tell myself that there hasn't been much opportunity, that the lighting has been bad, that I've been interrupted. And all those things are true, but I also know there's another reason: I'm stalling. I don't want to take some spectacular shot that Melissa will feel she has no choice but to run ASAP.

As I sit with my half-eaten lunch, I know there's really something wrong with me. I could have taken hundreds of shots if I'd wanted to. If I'd wanted to get them badly enough. Even if they turned out to be useless, I should have been taking them.

The trouble is, something's stopping me.

I take a swig from my bottle of water and glance at that something, who's sitting across the room from me: Ned.

This morning, after group (where, thankfully, the focus had been on Seth and his emotional breakthrough), I'd asked around about Ned, hoping to get that staccato-style story in three phrases or less. But no one knew all that much. A couple people thought it was father issues, a couple thought it was fame issues; no one thought he was here for anything like drugs or alcohol (which, again, confirmed Melissa's promise about the facility). Father issues would fall in line with what he'd told me last night, but everyone knew Matthew Hartnett left a lot to be desired. It was hardly breaking news.

"Jo?" An inmate I don't know taps me on the shoulder from behind, making me jump halfway to the ceiling. What is *wrong* with me? I'm never on edge like this.

"Yep?" I try to act something close to normal as I look up.

"There's a phone call for you. At the front desk. I think it's your mom?"

My eyebrows raise sky high when I hear this and I resist

the urge to jump up on the table and yell, "It's a miracle!" because I'm guessing it's my "other" mother—Melissa. And I'm sure she's right about ready to put me in the naughty corner.

I make my way out to the lobby, and the woman manning the front desk gestures to the phone I'm looking for. "Hello?" I say, picking up. I try not to sound too worried that she's calling.

"Jo. I need an update," a voice barks at me.

Oh yeah. That's Melissa, all right.

"The opportunities haven't been great," I say, by way of explanation. At least that's half the truth. There's no way I'm giving Melissa the other half—that my ability to point and shoot hasn't been all that great, either.

"Never stopped you before," Melissa answers.

"Well, I've got a couple of good . . . um, life-skills ideas," I suddenly change my wording at the last second as Katrina, Ned, and a few others pass by me and head for the front door. Katrina gestures toward the lake and I nod and hold up a "one minute" finger.

"What?"

"Sorry, people around," I say. "I got a couple passable shots this morning." I lower my voice to a whisper. "I'm hoping for some better ones this afternoon."

"That's a start, then. I've decided we've got to run with this soon, so the pressure's on. You have another day. Maybe two.

Three, tops. I'm following up some leads on the story, which will buy you some time. But make it snappy. You're not there to find yourself."

I should have known that nine days didn't mean nine days when it came to Melissa. "We're . . . ," I start, but then hear the dial tone. Guess that'll be it for our conversation. I end the call and pass the phone back. I'd been about to say we were set to go canoeing on the lake this afternoon, and I might be able to get a few more decent shots.

Maybe I can drown my guilt out there while I'm at it.

I can't risk taking my real camera down to the lake, even in my backpack, so I pat my fauxPod, still in my pocket from lunch, and follow the others outside.

It's a gorgeous day again—crisp, with a huge blue sky and white clouds drifting lazily past in the breeze. Perfect for canoeing. If you don't fall in, of course (I'm guessing there's probably no time of the year in Boston that you want to fall out of your canoe).

When I get down to the lake, everyone is already life jacketed, paired up, and in the water. After a second or two, Brad spots me and calls out. "I'll do a lap to get everyone going and then come back and swap with you, Jo."

I nod and wave. Fine by me.

I sit down on the bank and watch. Katrina and Ned have

paired up together, and despite all the splashing and laughing going on, they're actually doing really well. Katrina seems to have gotten her coordination together on the water just fine, and she and Ned have practically lapped some of the other people. In our room last night, in the dark, I'd started to add a few things together—Katrina telling me not to be "weird" about Ned when she was giving me the tour of the retreat, her tendency to be around him so much, the fact that she seemed to talk to him a lot more than many of the other people here—and I'd asked her if she was interested in him. A pillow had gone flying across the room. I took that as a definite "just friends."

As I watch them, I note the difference between Ned's expression last night and the one on his face now—he looks like he doesn't have a care in the world out there in that canoe. But last night, during our private talk, well, he's obviously pretty unhappy with his life right now. I wonder what's going on with him that's made his dad send him here.

Sitting in group today, I'd thought a lot about Brad's question—what would I change about my life? It's been haunting me. I can't seem to get it out of my head. What *would* I change? If I could, would I wish for a mother and a father and a brother, all housed behind that white picket fence? Maybe even a dog and a wood-paneled station wagon to really complete the look?

No, I don't think so.

Everyone seemed to think it's so weird that my dad is

away a lot when I don't have a mom around to look after me, but I've never questioned it that much. It's just how things *are*. Like they were the day before and will be the day after. That's Dad's big take on life: it is what it is. He's a literal kind of guy. Things are black and white in his world. It's all point and shoot. Anyway, it's hardly like anyone else here is "normal." If anyone is "normal" at all, even out in the real world.

What I'd told Ned was true, though. Spending just a small amount of time with him has made me realize I need to stick to my plans to get out of papping eventually and do my own thing. And I do have a plan that I'm following. Even though, right now, it isn't a plan I truly agree with.

Still, one thing's for sure—I'm not going to let Brad ask me any more questions that I don't have solid answers to. He's messing with my brain, bringing up things I don't need to be thinking about right now. And my brain doesn't like it. My brain had its nice little plan all worked out and . . .

Oh.

"Gotta run!" Katrina jumps out onto the bank and sprints past me with her long legs. "Too much soda at lunch!"

I watch her go.

"Jo! Come on, give it a try," Ned calls out, and I quit watching Katrina and turn back to look at him.

So much for that stellar "plan" of mine. Not one more shot taken.

I slip my shoes off and make my way down to the canoe, where I put on Katrina's vest. Before I know it, we've pushed off and are out on the water.

"Hey! I didn't fall in!" I say to Ned's back.

"You don't need to sound so surprised."

"I am surprised!" I tell him. "Sports and me . . . let's just say we don't mix well."

Ned stops paddling for a second and glances back at me. "But you did great at the circus workshop. You know, after you got down with dealing with us dirty, untrustworthy types."

I take my paddle out of the water now and give Ned a bit of a push in the back. I leave a satisfyingly large wet mark on his life jacket and even manage to get a few drips down his neck.

"Hey!"

"Watch it, or I'll tell Brad you've been bullying me. I'm delicate, you know."

Ned laughs. "I think you're the least delicate person I've ever met, Jo."

I snort. "Ha! I'll have you know I can be delicate."

He turns around slowly and gives me a look. I stick my tongue out. "Okay, so I can't be delicate. Actually, I kind of realized that the moment I got here, opened the shared closet, and saw Katrina's clothes."

Ned laughs again when I mention Katrina. "Did you see her run? She has really got to lay off the soda. She hasn't had any for years, and now she can't stop. Seriously, they should have halfway houses or something for ballerinas. She's lost touch with reality."

"Because of Sprite. That is a pretty sad teenage version of 'lost touch with reality.'"

"I'll say."

I pause for a second before I ask the question. "I guess you've seen a few people really lose touch . . . ," I say.

In front of me, Ned's shoulders visibly tense up. "I guess." He doesn't turn around.

I decide to let it go. I don't think I'll be getting a whole lot of information out of Ned. Probably best to avoid the fame bit from now on.

"So, you've got a brother . . . ," I say, trying a different line of questioning. And now Ned doesn't tense, he whips around, almost dropping his paddle in the water.

"How do you know I've got a brother?"

I freeze. He'd mentioned him. Last night. Hadn't he? I think back, fast. Oh, man. He hadn't. Think quick, Jo. Think quick. Or just lie.

"You mentioned him," I say. "Last night. When you were talking about your dad."

Ned pauses, his eyes flicking to the side, remembering. He doesn't look convinced. "Did I?"

I shrug, as if it's no big deal. "How else would I know?" Gee, I wonder . . . years of stalking the stars, maybe? "Katrina talks about her sisters all the time. I thought you could tell me about your brother. I don't have any siblings, so it's fun to hear about other people's." My stomach starts doing that awful squeezy thing again.

"Not much to tell, really." Ned turns around again and resumes paddling. "He lives in New York. We've got . . . very different lives."

"New York's not so far from Boston. Closer than LA, anyway. Have you managed to see him while you've been here?"

In front of me, Ned nods. But it seems nothing else is forthcoming.

"Katrina gets along with her sisters really well," I say, trying to lift the heavy mood in the canoe a little for fear it will sink us. "Or maybe that's just because she's been living away from them in New York for the last few years."

Cue comment from Ned.

Except that he misses his cue.

There's silence for the next few minutes, and I make the active decision to shut up, in the hope that Ned will start talking.

But he doesn't. And after a few more minutes, I start to look hopefully for Katrina. When is that girl coming back? In the end, I can't bear the silence any longer and have to say something. "That is one long pee!"

There's another pause in which the only sound is the water lapping at the side of our canoe. Then Ned laughs. "It really was a lot of soda."

"I guess so."

We paddle on in silence for a few more minutes until,

finally . . . *finally* . . . I see Katrina running down the hill toward the lake. "Here . . . ," I open my mouth to say, but, in the same moment, Ned is turning around to speak to me.

"Any other thoughts on what we talked about last night?" His eyes bore into me, brushing aside my words. Although I know exactly what he's talking about, I play dumb.

"Thoughts?" I try to look away, taken aback by the sudden intensity between us, but can't. It feels as if it would be almost impossible to break my eye contact with him.

Ned doesn't answer me, but he doesn't look away, either. He's not going to let this go, I can tell. "No," I tell him flatly. "I've been busy working on world peace."

He turns away then and starts paddling for the shore and the now-waiting Katrina. As we get closer, I speak up, realizing our time together is almost over. "What about you?"

He just shakes his head. "Trying to come up with a plan to fix the ozone."

Honestly, neither of us could sound more depressed if we tried. I think I might suggest to Brad that we all get some T-shirts made for Group B—T-shirts with a catchy little slogan on the front like . . .

LIFE: IT'S HARDER THAN IT LOOKS.

As we paddle in silence, I wonder why he brought up the subject again. It's like he was waiting to get me alone, like there's something weighing on his mind that he needs to tell someone about. A friend, or the closest thing he has to a friend in here. I watch his back for a moment or two, wondering about this. And then I find myself reaching out. I place my palm flat on Ned's back and he startles slightly.

I'm not sure what makes me do it. One second I was staring at his back and the next I was remembering the time his hand had been on me, when I was curled up in pain on those steps. And then my hand had reached out for him. Now, in front of me, Ned doesn't look around and he doesn't ask me what I'm doing.

After a while, I let my hand drop and I pick up my paddle again. Neither of us says anything about it.

I don't end up taking one single shot of Ned. I don't get a shot of him, his canoe, the lake, the trees . . .

I don't get one single shot of anything.

chapter 9

I can hardly believe it, but I start avoiding Ned after the canoe incident. Actually *avoiding* him. Which is so not like me. So not what my job is about. In fact, when you think about it, it's really the exact opposite of my job, isn't it? The one I'm being paid for, every second I'm here. The one I'm not doing.

The one Melissa will skin me alive for not doing.

When Katrina is in the shower after dinner, I take advantage of the quiet moment alone in our room to scroll through the shots I *do* have.

Well, there go three seconds of my life. I have maybe fifty half-decent shots in all. Embarrassing circus stuff, embarrassing circus stuff, embarrassing circus stuff, scarfing breakfast, scarfing lunch, scarfing dinner, coming out of group looking like he's picking his nose, of all things (which he wasn't, not that Melissa would care). Fifty shots altogether. That's just . . .

Pathetic, really.

Usually I take thousands of shots per day. And of course, thousands also get deleted, but the point is I *take* thousands. I know I'm working under difficult conditions, but they're also controlled conditions. I should have a whole lot of usable shots by now and a couple standout ones as well.

Something is wrong with me. Really, really wrong with me.

Brad's voice pops into my head then. "How about you, Jo? Is there something in particular you'd change?"

I throw my fauxPod in my backpack, as if it's red-hot, and jump up off the bed.

"Are you okay?" Katrina asks from the bathroom doorway.

"No," I shake my head. "I think Brad's gotten into my brain somehow."

Katrina nods slowly. "He's pretty good at doing that."

I frown. "So I've noticed. It's spooky."

A knock on the door makes us both turn. "Phone call for Jo," someone calls out, and then we hear footsteps as they walk away.

Katrina looks puzzled. "But it's not family phone call night."

Which can only mean one thing. Melissa. Only Melissa would be wily and conniving enough to get around the retreat's rules. Still, I can hardly blame her—if I were paying someone ten thousand plus dollars per day to be here, I'd be checking up on her, too, rules or no rules.

"You'd better go see who it is," Katrina urges me. "It must be important."

I sigh, a sigh that says, "Yeah, yeah," and silently trudge my way out the door, down the corridor, and stop at the front desk, where the woman manning it this evening passes me the phone.

"Hello?" I say warily.

"Jo, doll! How's it going?"

My eyebrows raise slightly. It's not Melissa, after all. It's the second wiliest and second most conniving person on earth.

"Dad?" I say. I wonder for a split second why he's calling me here and how he got the number, before I realize that though it's not Melissa on the phone, this still stinks of her. "So, Melissa's getting you to check up on me," I say with yet another sigh. "Do you think she calls all the paps' dads? Or am I just lucky?"

"You're just lucky, kid."

Suddenly, I go from slightly peeved to flaming angry in zero to three seconds. "I guess Melissa doesn't think I can do the job, then."

"I don't know. Can you?"

No. "Yes. Of course I can. Otherwise I wouldn't have taken it, would I?"

"Sounds like a pretty good job."

It bites. "It is."

"For what she's paying you, you'll never give up the game now."

I take a deep breath when I hear this. Here we go. Again. I take a second to turn around and lean my back on the large wooden front desk in the reception area. As I do, I see that my good friend Seth is now sitting in the lounge, half watching TV and playing with something that looks like a pen. "Yes, I will," I hiss into the phone. "That was the point of taking this job, which I actually think is pretty despicable. I'm not going to give up on going to school, Dad."

"Ah, sure, sure. I said the same thing twenty years ago," my dad replies. It's not that he's against me going to school. He's just against me not loving being a paparazzo as much as he does.

I shake my head at what I'm hearing. "Why do you always tell me I won't get out? Why is that so hard to believe? We're not the same person, are we?"

My dad just laughs. He never loses his cool, which just makes me lose mine more and end up looking like an over-excited idiot. "Jo, you're more like me than you think."

I want to make some comment about him having no choice but to say that, considering comparing my personality to my mom's wouldn't exactly be favorable, but I can't be bothered arguing about it. In the end, I don't say anything, though my silence on the matter says a whole lot. "How's Tokyo?" I finally ask halfheartedly, deciding changing the subject will expend less energy. I'm too tired to talk to my dad tonight. I just want to go to bed and forget about Melissa and Dad and Ned and . . . everything, really.

"Tokyo's great. You wouldn't believe how many stars are here on a daily basis making crappy commercials for truckloads of cash. And they don't like their fans in the US to know about it, either."

"I guess the sushi's good," I say, trying to remain neutral. I turn slightly again and then frown as I see something weird going on between Seth and Ned, who has just entered the scene, across the room.

"The sushi almost makes up for the apartment. I'm telling you, you couldn't swing a Nikon D3 in there."

I'm barely listening to him now, intent on what's happening in the lounge. After a year and a half of papping, I know a fight brewing when I see one, and that is exactly what's going down on the other side of the room. Seth is still sitting, kind of holding up the pen he'd been toying with before. Just a few paces away, Ned looks like a Rottweiler ready to pounce (and, believe me, I've seen that many a time, too. Thankfully, mostly from the *outside* of stars' gates).

"Hey!" Ned yells at Seth.

I grab the phone tighter in my hand. "Gotta go," I tell my dad. "Something's come up." My eyes not leaving Ned, I fumble to end the call and place the receiver back on the desk. I don't have to worry about him calling me back. We've ended calls to each other in this way at least a hundred times before.

"Hey, you! Seth!" Ned calls out again and takes a step or two forward.

113

Beside me, I can feel the woman at reception stand up. "What's going on?" she calls out to the two guys.

Ned glances over and then seems to remember himself and where he is. He looks odd. Really odd. Despite what's going on between him and Seth, I get that feeling again that he doesn't seem quite right. Very weird. "It's nothing." He waves a hand at the staff member. But his gaze remains sharply focused on Seth.

I head over to Ned and stand in between the two guys. "What's the matter?" I ask, looking from one to the other. I can't for the life of me see what Ned's problem is. Seth hadn't been doing anything exciting—simply sitting around and playing with a pen for something to do.

But Ned doesn't answer me. Instead he takes one step sideways so he can still see Seth. Or not Seth, I now realize. He hasn't really been looking at Seth all along—it's the pen he's interested in.

Seth gives him a look. "Do you have the same owner-ship issues she does?" He jerks a thumb in my direction. "How was I supposed to know the stupid pen was yours? It was just lying around here," he says, pointing to the coffee table.

"Sure. *If* it's a pen." Ned shakes his head, his jaw tight.

Seth's mouth twists. "You freak, of course it's a pen. Look, it's even got a little restful boat scene for all the insane people in here to stare at mindlessly." He holds it up now, and I can see what he's been doing—it's one of those pens with the

114

liquid-filled end and a little boat that you can move from one side to the other. Probably from some vacation spot.

"Prove it," Ned says, his face remaining tense.

"Prove it's a pen?" Seth shakes his head and stands up. "You really are nuts. You got out of Hollywood too late, you psycho." And with this, he twists the pen's body open and an ink cartridge falls out. It's as the ink hits the floor that I realize exactly what Ned's going on about, and all my internal organs freeze.

He's onto me.

"Satisfied, LA boy?" Seth says with a sneer as he stalks off past Ned.

Ned doesn't watch him go, just stands there and stares at where Seth had been. After a while, he groans slightly as his gaze moves to the ink cartridge on the floor.

As for me, I pick up the pieces of the pen and slowly put them together, trying to compose myself for what might be coming. When I'm done, I turn around to face Ned.

"What was that all about?" I ask him, trying to keep my tone even. After all, I know exactly what that was all about.

Ned just groans again. "Nothing. I . . . ," he starts, then shakes his head once more. The woman at the front desk is still watching us.

"Come outside." I grab his arm and pull him toward the front door. I'd better find out how much he knows. Or whether he's just guessing.

Ned doesn't object and lets me steer him out, where we

stand in the well-lit entrance, just off to the side of the front doors. It's cooler now and I can smell the pine trees again. Everything is fresh and crisp and I'm reminded we're a world away from the smog and the hard gray sidewalks of LA.

I give Ned a moment or two and it works. He finally runs one hand through his hair and exhales. "Seth's right. I am a psycho. He was holding a pen and I just . . . lost it. A pen!"

I watch him closely. "But why? What's up with the pen thing?" As if I don't know.

Ned looks down at me now, as if remembering that I'm even here. He stares for a second, seemingly trying to work something out. If he can trust me, maybe. "I . . ." He pauses, looking straight into my eyes. "I thought he was taking pictures."

"With a pen?" I say slowly.

"It was the way he was holding it up." Ned glances inside to where Seth had been sitting. "I thought it was a camera disguised as a pen. I hear there are some paparazzi out there who use things like that. Devices. Pens, fake iPhones. Stuff like that."

I can hear blood in my ears. "But iPhones have cameras in them . . . ," I say in an attempt to play dumb.

"No, I mean tricked out with a more sophisticated camera."

"Oh." I think over what Ned's saying, then pause for a second. "Weird." And what's definitely weird is that I'm standing before Ned Hartnett hearing all about the evil paparazzi. And even weirder, that while this is happening, pretty much all I can think about is how gorgeous he is.

116

"It *is* weird. Believe it or not, there are thirteen-year-old paparazzi out there."

"Oh," I say again, paying more attention now. It would be interesting to fill him in on how it really is, how the thirteen-year-olds who hang around are pretty much snot-nosed brats who fancy themselves the younger stars' best friends because they took a shot of them once. "Thirteen, huh?" I add, trying to sound like I'm slightly shocked. "What kind of parents must they have?" Probably ones like mine.

Ned exhales as he squints to see through the glass to the retreat's main building. "Look, Jo, I don't want to be rude or anything, but I might head back in. I'm not exactly the best company right now."

"Um, sure." I nod. "Of course. Have a good night. Get some rest."

"Yeah, you, too." Ned turns and heads inside.

I watch him go, practically seeing him in stills as he walks away. *Snap, snap, snap.* Unfortunately for Melissa, not one of those stills is real.

Surprisingly enough, I sleep okay for someone who's being paid thousands of dollars per day and is not doing her job. Seriously, sometimes I wonder about my conscience. Then again, if my personality is as close a match to my dad's as he thinks it is, maybe I never even had one in the first place.

I trudge out to breakfast and shovel in a bowl of cereal,

my eyes half-closed, my body unwilling, hardly believing I'm up at 8:00 a.m. I've been working all summer vacation and haven't gotten out of bed before 10:00 a.m. at home. Then again, I haven't crawled into bed until about 2:00 a.m., either. As I eat, Katrina sits down at my table, along with a few others from our group. Thankfully, it seems that pretty much nobody is one of those sick, cheery morning people, and so we eat mainly in silence.

"Good morning, everyone!" Brad bounces over and I chalk one up for the sick, cheery morning people. "Ready for a little jog?"

"No," someone answers.

"Oh, you know you all love it. Katrina? You're usually interested in getting some exercise."

"Sure," she says. "Count me in."

Katrina is too nice for her own good.

"Jo . . . ," Brad starts.

I glance up sharply, suddenly awake. I jog only to get absolutely prime shots. I do not jog for fun. No one jogs for fun. But before I can say anything, Brad continues.

"Now that you're all settled in, it's time for our first individual session this morning. I'll see you in ten minutes in my office. Everyone else, I'll wave as you jog past."

Once Brad leaves, I glance around the faces at the table. I have never wanted to go jogging so badly in my life.

chapter 10

"Come on in," Brad says when I knock hesitantly on his door, hoping and praying and wishing that in the twelve minutes that have just passed, he's magically forgotten our appointment and has run off somewhere to spread his morning cheer.

Sadly, it doesn't look like it.

"Um, thanks," I say, entering his office.

"Take a seat." He motions to a comfy-looking chair opposite him and, I'm sorry to say, not on the other side of a desk, or anything like that. This, I can see, is going to be a getting-inside-my-head half hour.

"No need to look so worried." Brad laughs slightly. "This is all very informal."

Yeah, right. I've gotten to know Brad a little since I've

been here, and while he might seem "informal," he's also very, very sneaky. I haven't forgotten the what-would-you-change? incident.

Brad spends a few minutes asking me about how I'm settling in and so on, and then, just as I'm letting my guard down slightly, he moves in for the kill. "I thought we could chat about the first workshop you did. The circus skills workshop."

Oh, great. And I'd been hoping we were past that.

"You did so well—"

"Let's cut to the chase," I say. "You want to talk about the trust thing. Again."

Brad laughs. "I like your directness, Jo."

"It saves a lot of time," I reply, then realize I'm not trying to save time here, I'm trying to kill it, and I really should have let him waffle until he was due somewhere else. Still, maybe it's better to get it over and done with. "It's like I said. I just think it's dumb to put people in a situation and tell them to trust each other. Not that I want to argue about it again," I add quickly.

Brad nods slowly. "I see your point. And, yes, these sorts of activities can be a tad artificial, I do agree . . ." I wait for the "but."

"But . . . ," Brad starts again. I knew it. "They can also highlight some of our character traits. You're very independent, aren't you, Jo?"

I shrug. "I guess. I have to be, don't I?" Brad's more than aware that my mother is out of the picture (I wonder what he'd make out of that paparazzo pun if he knew the real deal about me) and my father is currently flying back and forth between two countries a couple times a month. And how glad am I now that I decided to go with the truth? I would have been better off pretending to be the child of Melissa—vicious newspaper editor by day and celebrity bloodsucker by night.

"You're right, of course. You do need to be independent in a situation like yours. But what I want to talk about is how you *feel* about that."

I shrug again. "What's the point? It is what it is," I use my dad's line. "Anyway, it doesn't matter how I feel about it, because it's just the way things are. Nothing's going to change."

Brad pauses for a second and we stare at each other intently. Finally, he speaks. "But that's the thing, Jo. You see, it does matter. Because it matters to *me* how you feel about it. And that changes everything."

As I shut Brad's office door behind me, I shake my head slightly. You've got to give it to the man—he is a master. Within the space of the past twenty minutes, he'd managed to get me to acknowledge that it did matter how I felt about my existence. That maybe it was okay to come out and say I got a bum deal. He'd weaseled the basics of my mom's story out of me (that she'd dumped me on my dad on day three of my life and run off). And then he'd somehow gotten me to admit that my dad didn't provide the best means of bringing up a kid—how he went through an endless array of babysitters and nannies and then, when I was old enough, started traveling overseas every couple of weeks, leaving only my cousin to watch out for me. "It is what it is" might have worked from my dad's point of view, but it didn't necessarily work from mine. And Brad wasn't looking for me to feel sorry for myself, or to cry and rant and wail and ask my dad to come home, but just to say, "Hey, I deserve better than what I was served up."

And the weird thing is, as I walk away from Brad's office, I actually feel kind of good for being able to think this. Because I know I did and still do deserve better. And, like I'd told Ned the other night, that's what I'm working toward—carving out my own life. I remember my dad's words now, about me not wanting to get out after I've been paid the big bucks for this job.

Well, he's wrong. Flat-out wrong.

If there's one thing I'd gotten out of Brad's and my little chat, it was a reminder that I'm getting older and wiser. And, as I get older and wiser, I gain control. *I* control my life and *I* control what I do.

And what I'm going to do is get through this Melissa business. I'm going to get through it and get out on the other side—where I'll have a completely different life.

All I have to do now is take the shots Melissa needs, which will set me straight on the path I want: to school.

So get on with it then, I tell myself as I start back toward my room with a steely resolve. *Get on with it and get out of here.*

★ ★ ★

After everyone's back from their jog and showered, we have two choices for the rest of the morning—pottery class or nature walk. Ned chooses pottery, so I do, too. I then sprint to room 20 to grab my fauxPod. While I'm there, I spot my faux-glasses as well and decide to bring them—you never know, we might end up outside for a minute or two. Then I meet back up with the rest of the group as they make their way to the art center.

As it turns out, the art center is in a separate building behind the main block, attached to it by an elevated bridge. In job mode, I scope out the area as we make our way inside. Unfortunately for me, the whole place is sort of elevated. I think it might be some kind of architectural design meant to bring in light, because the entire art center is practically made of glass. It's beautiful, but it immediately puts being outside and shooting through a window out of the question. So, from inside the room it is.

Brad hands us over to the art coordinator, Ellen, who leads us into the room we'll be using for today's class. The first thing I notice is that the large windows provide good light and plenty of it. I also register that there's a choice of eight pottery wheels. I wait until Ned chooses and then take the one that will give me the best view of him and what he's doing. There are good prospects for some shots here. Some decent shots this morning, combined with the circus skills shots, will keep Melissa off my back for at least twenty-four hours for sure.

I can do this, I tell myself, touching my fauxPod in my pocket, just to make sure it's still there. It is. How I'm going to get away with using it, I have no idea, but I'm going to have to somehow. My fauxglasses I hang off the neck of my T-shirt. I guess if I get desperate I can use them. Since the room is pretty sunny, the shots would be okay.

Over the next half hour or so, Ellen gives us a quick tutorial on how to throw the clay down, center it, open it, pull up the walls, and then trim the base. After this, she gives us all a portion of clay and we're supposed to get down to business. The thing about pottery, I quickly find, is that it is a whole lot harder than it looks. When Ellen does it, it all seems very simple. Soothing, even.

It's not. The clay is rougher than I'd expected and the whole process is dirtier, too. I still have no idea how I'm going to get my fauxPod out of my pocket and take shots of Ned without smearing clay all over the lens. I glance down at my fauxglasses and shrug to myself. I'll look like an idiot, but that's happened before. With dirty fingers, I pick them off my T-shirt, flick them open, and put them on. Seemingly adjusting them, I press the silver stud on the right hand side and take a shot of Ned. Then another.

"Looking very rock star, Jo," Katrina says from her seat right beside me, making me glance over.

"It's a little sunny in here," I say just as a cloud moves across the sky and the room darkens slightly. "Or it was."

"Okay," Katrina replies. But when I look around the room again, I realize it's not just Katrina who thinks my indoor shades are a little odd. With a sigh, I take them off and stick them back on my T-shirt. It'll have to be the fauxPod. Again.

I pay attention to my pottery for a while until Katrina gives me an idea. Her first piece doesn't go well and Ellen ends up giving her more clay. Katrina dumps the first piece on a large sheet of paper that's sitting on the floor beside her, and it's as I watch the clay hit the floor that the idea comes to me. As fast as I can, I wreck mine too by making a well in it that's far too deep and ask if I can try again as well.

And then, when no one's looking and everyone's assuming I'm busy with that second piece of clay, I get out my fauxPod, dump it in the well of the first piece of clay, and make the best makeshift fake pottery camera the world's probably ever seen.

★ ★ ★

For the next hour, everyone messes around with their clay and their potter's wheel. So do I, by the looks of things, but what I'm really doing is switching between my two pieces whenever possible. Despite all my just-do-it bravado, I still have to talk myself into taking further pictures of Ned, even though they're not the first ones of the day. It doesn't make any sense, but the more I shoot, the harder it is to keep going. The truth, I realize after a while, is that I'm disgusted. Disgusted at taking the shots, disgusted at not taking more shots. Disgusted at being here, disgusted at still being here, and prolonging the agony when I could already be gone. The reason I'm disgusted with myself changes from minute to minute, but the feeling remains.

After what I hope are twenty usable shots, I have to get up and leave the room. I mutter something to Katrina about the bathroom as I go, in case anyone wonders, but what I really do is stop just outside the entrance and kick one of the metal pylons holding the place up. I hate this so much. And what is my problem, really? I decided to take this job, didn't I? Now I should just get on with it and then run back to LA.

I move over to the other side of the connecting bridge and peer into the pottery room. My eyes are instantly drawn to Ned.

I stare at him for I don't know how long. It could be seconds, it could be minutes or hours. I stare until I'm so filled with self-loathing that I pull back and kick one of the metal pylons again. And again and again and again.

Him. Ned. That's what's wrong with me. I've gotten to know him far too well. That was my first big mistake—not keeping my distance. I should have played Hoodie Boy's trick and just slunk around in the background looking surly.

The thing is, when you don't know them, it's easy to chase stars down, hang around them when they've told you to get lost, invade their personal space, find out what kind of coffee they just ordered or what kind of face wash they bought at the drugstore when another company is paying them millions to promote something else. It's not difficult at all when they mean nothing to you other than where your next paycheck is coming from. When you can see them as little more than a way to get the money you need for school. But I can't see Ned like that anymore. The thing is, I've come to like him.

Too much.

Okay, fine. Way too much.

That's what's making this so hard. And I don't *want* to like him. I want Ned to be an evil, nasty, bitter, and twisted star who squishes wads of chewed gum into my hair that I have to cut out at 3:00 a.m. when I get home. I want him to make it easy to take invasive photos of him recovering from the hardships of stardom in fancy retreats. But he's not making it easy for me. He's not making it easy at all. He's picking me up off the ground before I even know him and then, when I do get to know him, he's still supportive and nice and—

"Jo?" The door pushes open to reveal Ellen. "Everything okay?" she asks, looking concerned.

"Just getting some air. Everything's fine," I tell her and

push off from the railing to follow her inside. Sure. Everything's fine. Everything's just freakin' fantastic.

★ ★ ★

I manage to take another five photos or so as everyone finishes up with their pieces and then just kind of sit and stare into space, trying not to think about anything much.

"Jo? Both of yours in the kiln, or just the one?" I look up to see Ellen hovering above me.

I glance at both pieces. The first piece is a misshapen mound of fauxPod-enclosed clay. The second is a sad attempt at a vase. For one crazy second, I think about putting both of them in the kiln. Maybe even accidentally flicking my faux-glasses in there as well. That would certainly solve a lot of my problems, though none of the Melissa-based ones. "Just the vase," I tell her. "I might take this one with me, if that's okay. You know, keep playing around with it . . ."

"Sure, of course," Ellen says, moving on to Katrina and her pieces.

Yup, might be a good idea to take the piece of clay with the fifteen-hundred-dollar camera inside it.

"Ready for lunch?" Katrina is wiping her hands off on a towel beside me.

I nod. Sure, why not? I may even manage to get some photos of Ned eating bacon bits. I'm sure that'd make Melissa's lead page.

chapter 11

I skulk around in the afternoon, keeping pretty much to myself during lunch, going for a walk afterward and lying low in group. After group, I take another walk by myself and snap a single shot of a squirrel with my now cleaned-up fauxPod.

Yes, a squirrel.

These are desperate times.

I scrounged a minute or two alone in our room before lunch, where I managed to download the shots I'd taken in the pottery studio. The few from my sunglasses were okay, but nothing all that hot. There were two from the fauxPod that were almost usable. I couldn't tell how much was of poor quality because the camera was encased in clay and how much was me not having the heart to take them in the first place.

Now, I go back to room 20 again and, for something to do, download the squirrel shot.

It is eerily good.

This, combined with a passing thought of having it Photoshopped to add in his own pair of dark sunglasses and call him a "celebrity squirrel," depresses me even further, and I lurk in our room until dinner with a "headache," eat dinner (again, pretty much in silence), and then head back to the room to lurk some more and read Katrina's magazines. I know I should be following Ned around, but I don't really care.

Halfway through a magazine, there's a knock on the door. I get up unwillingly and open it to find someone standing there whom I really don't want to see.

"Nine to ten again tonight," Rowan says, with a nod.

"Yeah, whatever," I say, closing the door on him with a bang. I don't have the energy this evening to come up with any sass.

I slump back on the bed once more, knowing that I am dangerously close to losing this job. It feels as if I'm clinging on to the edge of a cliff. And while part of me wonders whether it would be a relief for it all to be taken away, there's another part of me that knows I'm holding on to the job with the very tips of my fingernails, scared to let go and fall. Because I can't lose this job. There's no other big job to save me at the bottom. Just a whole lot more of long nights of papping and falling asleep at school. I need to dig in and hope I can pull myself up over the side somehow.

When I've flicked through every single one of Katrina's magazines and identified at least four of my own shots, I put the last magazine on the pile I've made on the floor and flop back onto my bed with a sigh.

"You're practically institutionalized and it's only day three." Katrina comes out of the bathroom rubbing her hair with a towel. "You need to do something before you go insane."

"Too late," I moan.

"Seriously," Katrina continues, "I mean it. You need to get out of this room."

"And do what?" I roll over to look at her. "It's almost eight. Scary curfew time. No going out of the doors after that, or the bogeyman will come and get me. Or Brad will come and get me. Not sure what's worse, actually."

Katrina laughs. "Me, either." She pauses for a second or two, thinking. "Why don't you go for a quick swim? You haven't been yet, have you? Apparently it counts as being officially indoors, so you can do that until nine.'

I think about her suggestion for a second. It's not a bad idea. "Have you heard if anyone else is going tonight?"

Katrina nods. "I think Ned and a couple other guys were, but they usually go before dinner. If you want to swim alone, you should be safe now. But the pool does close at nine, like I said, so if you really want to, you'd better hurry."

I take Katrina's advice, and within minutes I've pulled on

my swimsuit, wrapped my towel around my waist, and put on a sweatshirt over my top. A swim will be perfect. Just what I need—lap after lap of counting stroke after stroke. My thoughts wiped clear with excessive chlorination. Maybe I'd even figure out some fantastic excuse to tell Melissa tonight.

When I get to the pool door, I peep through the glass to see if there are any stragglers around. None. There's a towel that's been left behind, but not a person in sight. Relieved, I enter and throw my towel and sweatshirt on the long steel bench that runs the length of the pool. Then I take the few steps over to the deep end and dive in. Probably the most me-like action I've taken today. I'm not a testing-the-water type of person. I mean, you're going to get in, right? Get in already and quit with the fussing around.

I do one full lap of the pool, flip turn, then head back. Stroke, stroke, stroke. I feel better already. When I reach the wall, I do another flip turn and head back. And I'm thinking I must almost be at the wall again when I open my goggle-less eyes to check if I'm right and realize there are legs. There are legs in my lane. In front of me. With a jolt, I stop swimming and stand up.

"Excuse me," Ned says. "But I think you stole my lane."

I look to my left and then to my right. There are five other lanes, all empty.

So what is Ned Hartnett doing in mine?

I decide to play along. "Your lane?" I put a hand on one hip.

Ned nods. "Yes, *my* lane. And there," he gestures with one hand, "is my towel. You'll notice, at the foot of *my* lane."

Oh. So it wasn't an abandoned towel at all. It was Ned's towel.

"You leave your towel in a specific spot to guard your lane?"

"When I have to pee, yes." He grins. "Or would you rather I peed in the pool?"

I'm silent for a second. And so is Ned.

"I think we're starting to talk too much about peeing." He grimaces slightly. "First Katrina's soda issues and now my pool ones."

I nod in agreement.

"I think I'll let you have the lane, after all," Ned continues. "As I believe that may have been too much information about bodily functions."

"It was." I nod, trying not to laugh. "But if it makes you feel any better, you'll note I'm still in the water. For future reference, if you told me what kind of soda you drank too much of and how it meant you had to exit the pool to pee, I'd probably get out."

"Good to know," Ned replies, ducking under the lane rope. "Now, I'll race you to the end and back. If I get there first, the lane's mine," he says quickly, and before I know it, he's pushed off from the wall.

"Hey!" I start, but realize I'm protesting for nothing and crouch down and push off the wall myself. *Cheat*, I think, as

I swim faster and faster, gasping for air. At the end of my first lap, I flip turn and notice I'm not that far behind Ned at all. That's the beauty of growing up in California with a beach-loving Aussie father: you swim better than everyone else. As I keep swimming my second lap, I open my eyes to check once, then twice for the wall. And I'm almost there and am checking for a third time, reaching my arm out, when I reach it right out and into Ned, who's in my lane once again.

I begin to stand up, dripping wet and confused, when something even more confusing happens. Ned pulls me the rest of the way up, and before I know it . . .

He's kissing me.

And even more confusing . . .

I'm kissing him back.

It all happens so suddenly, I don't even have time to recover my breath from our race. Or maybe it's just that I lose it again. I almost think I'm imagining what's going on—that maybe I've accidentally dived into the pool at the shallow end and hit my head, or sucked up a lungful of water some-how and drowned (and am in heaven, obviously). After all, I've been imagining this moment at least half of every minute that I've been in Ned's presence. Now it's actually happening. His lips on mine—warm compared to the cool water we're standing in.

And sure, I've been kissed before, but not like this. Not in the way that the event itself is better than the ideal I dreamed up.

I expect Ned to pull back at any second. To say, "Wait up. I've got the wrong person here. Sorry, wrong lane." Or I expect me to end it. Because what I'm doing—kissing a star—goes contrary to everything I've been brought up to believe. It goes against my job description and common sense and any possible way of doing the task that I'm here to do.

But I don't care.

I don't care because I now realize that I've wanted to do this so very badly from the very first second Ned reached out and dragged me and my aching elbow up from those concrete stairs and, well, cared.

Ned Hartnett. *I'm kissing Ned Hartnett* is all my chlorine-soaked brain can think, over and over again, as my lips explore his. I'm kissing Ned Hartnett. Ned Hartnett. I'm kissing Ned Hartnett and he's kissing me. We're kissing each other. Me and Ned Hartnett.

It's so odd. Yet, at the same time, it feels just right. Like it was meant to happen all along, ever since that first evening we'd met. That if we hadn't ended up doing this, one of us might have spontaneously combusted.

Finally, when I need to breathe, I pull back.

"What are you doing?" I start.

Ned laughs, then grins and finally shrugs.

I watch him and start shaking my head slightly. It's his shrug, however, rippling across his muscles, making his torso move in front of me, that jogs something in my memory. I remember that other night again—the one outside his house when he was sick—and frown. I'd been thinking about it on the minibus back from the circus skills workshop. Ned had been in pain with appendicitis, and I'd taken those very lucrative shots of his bare top half outside his house.

The thing with Ned was that all the paparazzi knew where he lived but never bothered to go out there. It was like Willy Wonka's chocolate factory: no one ever went in and no one ever went out. Well, except for big black SUVs with tinted windows that you couldn't get a shot through. For all we knew there could have been Oompa Loompas living there along with Ned and his father.

But that night, something completely unexpected happened, and I was the first to get there and the only person who got any shots. It had been my dad who got the tip-off from a friendly EMT—there'd been an ambulance sent out to Ned's place. For Ned himself. But Dad had been busy on the other side of town and I was less than a five-minute cab ride away.

When I got there, the ambulance was just pulling up, so I found myself a good spot by a hedge and waited.

It didn't take long—I think Matthew Hartnett must have already been walking Ned down to the gate. Ned had one arm around his dad's neck, and Matthew was kind of supporting him as they made their way slowly down the drive toward the flashing lights.

That's when I started flashing some lights of my own. With no one else around to steal the show, I got some fantastic shots of father and son, shots of the EMTs taking over from Matthew Hartnett, and then shots of Ned as the EMTs helped him into the ambulance.

My forehead wrinkles now as I remember those shots. I recall thinking at the time that Ned didn't look right. There was something odd about his face. Like I'd said the other day, I chalked it up to the pain. I mean, the guy was almost doubled over. He'd looked at me as he walked past. Really looked into my camera. And even though those probably would have been the best shots of the night, for some reason, I stopped and dropped my camera, shocked at what I was taking photos of—someone in serious pain. Someone who needed surgery.

It wasn't one of my finest moments.

Now, still frowning, I look down Ned's body, taking in his chest properly. He's definitely more muscular and heavier than that night I'd been outside his house, but that's not surprising. Stars' bodies are generally all over the place, depending on their work schedule. A star can be all rippling muscles for a film one minute and then downing cheeseburgers the next, once their work in the role has ended. And while Ned had been mostly at home, for all I knew, he could have had a personal trainer coming in every day. His top half duly inspected, my eyes travel farther down his skin, to the very edge of his swimsuit that's riding just above the water's edge.

And that's when I spot something, or don't spot something

as the case may be, and move into work mode. I forget about any kissing, Ned Hartnett or otherwise (not that there's been a lot of otherwise, but still . . .). My hand whips out and pulls his waistband down slightly.

Nothing.

"What are you doing?" He repeats my question, now looking as confused as I was seconds ago.

I let his waistband snap back and stand up tall.

"I don't know," I tell him, a surge of adrenaline making my heart beat a whole lot faster than kissing him had. "But I think you should consider answering my question first, whoever you are, because I know one thing for sure—you are *not* Ned Hartnett."

chapter 12

Not-Ned laughs again, but this time it's a nervous laugh. "What do you mean I'm not Ned Hartnett?"

I take a step back from him. "I mean," I repeat, "you're not Ned Hartnett. That seems like a pretty clear statement to me."

Not-Ned opens his mouth, shuts it again, and then I see his jaw harden. He looks away for a moment or two. When he turns back again, it's with narrowed eyes. "You're crazy."

"Am I?" I don't move my eyes from his. At least now I know I'm really *not* crazy. Those moments where I'd had this sense that something was up with Ned Hartnett—that something wasn't quite right about him, that he looked different, or a bit off—well, this is why. There was no crazy amount of Photoshopping on his shots, there was no nose job, he didn't look different that night at his house because he was sick.

He looked different because it wasn't him.

There were two Ned Hartnetts around the place—the real one that I'd seen entering the ambulance, doubled in pain, and this one. The one that had picked me up off those concrete steps and lectured me about lying low.

The one that was standing right in front of me. My guess? That the guy I've just kissed is either some kind of amazingly good Ned Hartnett impersonator or Ned's brother.

No, he's too alike. It's *got* to be his brother. Maybe even a twin. And a brother or a twin who's been standing in for him for some time now. Maybe even for years.

There's a long pause where I can almost hear the options clanging against each other in Not-Ned's brain—to tell or not to tell? Run? Sprint? Freeze? Hide? Finally, I decide just to get it right out there in the open between us. "You're his brother, right?" I figure I'd never heard anything about a twin, but I'd definitely heard he had that brother in NYC.

He unfreezes now and turns and lifts himself out of the pool. He starts toward his towel. I guess he decided on "run."

"Hey!" I yell. "Don't think you're going anywhere." I lift myself out of the pool and chase after him. "I want some answers!"

Not-Ned picks up his towel and starts drying himself off, ignoring me.

I reach him and try to grab the towel that's drying off his hair. "Stop! You heard me!"

He yanks his towel back. "Answers? About what? Like I told you, you're crazy."

"Don't bet on it," I tell him. "Where's your scar then? From the appendectomy you had last year?"

He glances down his right-hand side uncertainly. "Plastic surgery. It's amazing what they can do these days."

Now I laugh. "Wrong, bozo. It's all keyhole surgery now. You should have three tiny scars, not one big one. So, are you going to tell me now I'm not so crazy? Who are you really? And what are you doing here? Where's the real Ned Hartnett?"

There's another long pause, but in it I can see that I've really got him now. He knows I know that he's definitely not Ned. "I . . . ," Not-Ned starts, but then the door to the pool opens up, interrupting us.

It's Brad.

"Sorry, guys, time to close," he says, looking from one of us to the other. "Everything okay?"

I nod. "*Ned* and I were just doing a few laps. Weren't we, *Ned*?"

"Sure," Not-Ned agrees a little too heartily.

"Great!" Brad nods. "Well, if you've got everything, I'll turn the lights off."

"Not a problem." I grab my towel and wrap it around me, then grab the guy's arm and pull him toward the door. "We were just going, anyway. See you in the morning, Brad!"

"Yes, see you," Brad says, and gives us an odd look as we pass by, and I can tell he'll be asking around in the morning to see if there's something going on between us.

Huh. Five minutes ago, maybe. Now? Not likely.

We head down the carpeted corridor and I keep dragging until we reach a doorway. Small as I am, I shove Not-Ned inside into the half dark. I'm about to start demanding answers when I realize I'd like to demand other things as well. I pull back from him a little then, scared that I actually might. "Well," I say gruffly, "are you going to tell me what's going on?"

He wraps his towel around his waist tighter now and tucks it in before he acknowledges me. When he sees the expression on my face, he laughs slightly. "Or what? You'll step on my foot? Kiss me to death?"

Mind on the job. Mind on the job. I ignore that last comment and try not to let my serious expression waiver. "Information," I tell him coolly, "is power."

He loses his slight smile with this and finally says to me, "I'm not some kind of freak pretending to be Ned Hartnett. It's not just me who has something to lose here."

I watch him closely. Interesting. So, whatever this is about, I now have confirmation that it does actually have something to do with the real Ned Hartnett and isn't just a case of some "weirdo brother's cry for help." Instantly, my mind whirs into overdrive. The strongest theory I have is "cover-up."

"So where's the real Ned?" I ask as noises start up

down the corridor—doors closing, lights being switched off. Brad.

Not-Ned hears it, too. "We have really got to get back to our rooms. I need to stay at this retreat, and I'm guessing you're not looking to be thrown out, either." His eyes challenge mine.

"No. I'm not."

Down the corridor, another door closes with a bang.

"Don't get any ideas," he says quickly. "It's not what you're thinking. No drugs, no alcohol, nothing like that."

Bang!

"Meet me tomorrow morning. Before breakfast. Down by the lake," he continues. "And I'll tell you what's going on. Now, go. Before Brad catches us and we get a repeat of the Spanish Inquisition."

★ ★ ★

"Good swim?" Katrina lowers her magazine to look at me as I enter room 20.

"Oh yeah," I nod. "Best swim I ever had."

"Cleared your head?"

Cleared my head? Um, not exactly. Instead of being lovely and clear, my head is now buzzing. There's no way I'll be sleeping tonight. "Mmmm," I answer Katrina.

"Oh, I almost forgot. There was another note for you. Here you go." She sits up and fishes it off her bedside table.

This brings me down to earth. It's probably from Melissa.

Melissa of 9:00 p.m. to 10:00 p.m. I take the note from Katrina. My eyes skim it quickly. And, *phew,* it's not from Melissa at all.

"It's from Wendy," I say, looking up. "Just checking in again. She's in London. She says, 'Any problems, just call.'" I have the urge to run out to the phone, wrestle it from whoever is manning the desk, and get Wendy to fly over and sort out this whole mess. She could do it, too, she's that kind of person. No one messes with Wendy.

But no . . . I made this now-even-more-complicated mess and, somehow, I have to find a way out of it. I crumple the note in one hand. "Um, I might just take a quick shower," I say. And before Katrina can reply, I make my way into the bathroom and close the door behind me.

My mind jumps from one crazy theory to the next as I turn the shower on, strip down, and get in. As I rinse away the chlorine, the phrase "cover-up" repeats itself over and over. But Not-Ned had made it clear that whatever was being covered up, it wasn't about drugs or alcohol. So what was it? A girl? A bad album? A split from his recording company? And why have Not-Ned at a retreat? No one knows he's here, anyway . . . Well, except for Melissa. And me.

However hard I try, I can't make the pieces of the jigsaw puzzle fit together. Though maybe that would be easier if I could divert all of my brain cells away from focusing on that kiss. If only it hadn't been so annoyingly . . . perfect.

The more I think about the whole Ned/Not-Ned thing, the

less it starts to make sense. As I let the water flow over me, the thought passes fleetingly through my mind that maybe I should call my dad, but I dismiss it almost immediately. No way. Wouldn't he just love that? Me, in a bind, asking him for papping advice. No, I couldn't give him the satisfaction.

By the time I've dried off, put on pj's, and brushed my teeth, I've managed to slow down my buzzing brain. It actually became a lot easier once I replaced Ned in a certain memory of mine with Seth (instant turnoff). I'll have to remember that trick. It's amazingly effective.

With a deep breath, I open up the bathroom door and Katrina places her magazine on her bedside table. "You're popular tonight," she says. "*Another* message came for you while you were in the shower."

"Really? Where is it?"

Katrina shakes her head. "Sorry, I meant a verbal message. It was a bit cryptic, actually."

"Cryptic?"

"Well, the guy said it was from a 'Melissa' and she needed any 'life skills ideas' you have. Urgently."

"Oh."

"Does that make sense to you?"

"Yeah," I say. "Unfortunately, it makes perfect sense."

★ ★ ★

After some good, hard thinking, I send Melissa something—an e-mail. In it, I tell her things are just getting interesting and that the shots will be ready by tomorrow. I attach the photo of the squirrel, however, telling her the scenery is beautiful. Just to annoy her.

I did consider sending the shots. Especially since I now know there's some kind of game being played here. What stopped me is that I'm not sure what it is, or who it's being played on. And I want to find that out first before I send Melissa anything.

By seven thirty the next morning, I am down by the lake, waiting for Not-Ned. Seeing as it's summer and all, I hadn't thought to bring even a light sweater. But then I'd forgotten I wasn't in California anymore and that it was getting close to fall.

Stupid Boston. Why couldn't these people all "find themselves" in a warmer place, like Hawaii? Hawaii would have been perfect.

After what feels like forever, but is probably about fifteen minutes, I get my first glimpse of Not-Ned approaching and the exact thing I'd been hoping wouldn't happen, happens. I get this jolt straight through me and have to think about kissing Seth again. As Not-Ned gets closer, I hold my breath, not wanting to smell him. See? That's how messed up I am. I can't believe I just thought about smelling him. That's weird.

When Not-Ned reaches me, he doesn't say anything, or even acknowledge my presence, he simply grabs my arm and keeps walking, pulling me behind a large tree.

Somehow, I get the feeling there won't be any kissing

going on during this meeting. "Oh yeah, good idea," I say, tugging my arm away and hoping my cheeks aren't coloring, because I'm sure I'm the only person here who was even slightly hopeful that something other than talking was going to happen between us. "Because everyone else is going to suddenly feel like a quick paddle in a canoe right about now and we'll be completely exposed." He gives me a look and I cross my arms in response. "So?" Now that we're on track, I am all about the professionalism. I am here for one thing and one thing only—the truth. And he'd better make it snappy.

In front of me, Not-Ned sighs. But it's more of an I-don't-know-where-to-start sigh than anything else. "Start anywhere," I tell him. "Maybe even with your *real* name."

"I guess that's as good a place as any." He smiles a small, reluctant smile. "Hi, I'm Jake," he says, "Ned's older brother."

"Nice to meet you, Jake." My voice drips with sarcasm. Always nice to finally find out the real name of someone I've already kissed. "Anything else you'd like to add, perchance?"

He opens his mouth, then closes it again. I decide to prompt him. "Okay, so you're the brother who lives in New York, right? You must be pretty close in age."

"I'm eighteen months older," Jake continues. "Our parents split when we were about twelve. Ned was working, of course, so he stayed with our father in LA. I chose to live with my mom and move back closer to her family in New York."

"You could be twins." I give him a slow once-over. "Or maybe not. How long have you been covering for him?" I try

147

to remember the last time I saw Ned Hartnett actually sing in the flesh and can't recall how many years it's been. He's made appearances—on TV, on the red carpet, and so on—but any of those appearances could have been Jake pretending to be Ned. For all I know, those rumors about Ned weighing five hundred pounds and being stuck in his house could well be true.

Jake raises an eyebrow. "We're very alike, but not close enough. Obviously. And how long have I been covering for him? Not that long. Two years, tops. And only every now and then. I can't believe you noticed. No one has before." He shakes his head.

I watch him for a second or two before I respond. "I . . . tend to notice things."

Jake laughs slightly at this. "So you're a bit of a Ned Hartnett fan, are you?"

I think back to the night Ned had been taken away by the ambulance and realize now that it had been my one true sighting of him—*Ned* Ned. The real one. But the Ned Hartnett who'd picked me up off those concrete steps had been *Jake* Ned. And then I feel my face get hot as I realize the truth of my secret star crush.

I'm not a bit of a Ned Hartnett fan.

I'm a bit of a Jake Hartnett fan.

It had been Jake who picked me up off the ground. And it had been Jake doing those fake faints the other night, too. Pretty much anytime I'd taken shots of Ned Hartnett, I'd been taking shots of Jake. Except for the night of the ambulance. No wonder Jake was getting away with pretending to be Ned. As far as the public was concerned, he *was* Ned.

"Where's the real Ned, then?" I ignore Jake's embarrassing fan question.

Jake looks over the expanse of still, cold water. And at the ground. And at the sky. "Um . . ."

"Come on," I say. "You know you're going to have to tell me. And I don't think you're a very good liar, to tell the truth. You may as well just come out with it."

He looks back at me. "I don't think you're going to believe me when I tell you."

"Try me," I say. "You might be surprised."

There's a pause as Jake stares at me, almost as if he's trying to gauge whether he can trust me or not. And I don't know whether he decides he can or can't or simply realizes it's pointless wondering about whether he can or can't, because I'm all over what he's up to, anyway, but he does decide to keep talking. "He's still in LA," he says quietly. "In a psychiatric hospital. Getting treatment for a phobia."

As Jake stares at me, waiting for my reaction, I deliberately don't give him one. Instead, I take the information in. I digest it. And when it gets all the way down to my gut, I find that my gut doesn't reject it but instantly believes what he's telling me. Jake is telling me the truth here, the truth about what is really going on with his brother.

"That's why I'm here," Jake rushes in before I can reply.

"I'm the decoy. In case anyone goes looking too hard for Ned, I'm him—getting some rest from stardom." He doesn't sound too impressed with this plan, which piques my interest, because if he doesn't want to be here, why is he here at all?

I frown, a couple things not adding up for me at this point, but I decide to let Jake keep going with his story, and when he's done, I'll see how things tally at the end. But Jake seems to have stopped. "What kind of phobia?" I finally prompt him.

"I was afraid you might ask that," he says.

No. Really? As if I wouldn't.

Jake bends down and picks up a pebble. I watch as he steps forward and throws it, skimming it across the lake. It skips five times.

"Whenever you're finished showing off your Boy Scouts skills . . . ," I say as he reaches toward the ground again. "I'm guessing you aced your impersonation badge."

He stands upright once more. "Fine. Ned has . . ." He hesitates. "It's . . . Ned has a problem with . . ." He stalls again.

"Jake," I butt in. "Please. Just get it over and done with. I'm starving. I'm starting to get very bored. Ned has a problem with . . ."

Jake sighs another one of his sighs. Poor guy. He's probably never sighed so much in his life before he met me. "Crowds," he finally answers, running one hand through his hair. "Ned has a problem with crowds."

chapter 13

I laugh when Jake tells me this. I actually laugh out loud. "You know the part where you said I wouldn't believe you?"

"Yes."

"Well, I don't believe you," I say, and laugh again, maybe even louder this time. "Ned Hartnett has a crowd phobia? Come on . . ." Now I really think this *is* about drugs. Or alcohol. Or both.

I take the opportunity to quiz him on the other stuff that doesn't make sense to me. "So, what you're telling me is you're pretending to be Ned in a retreat so that no one guesses Ned is in a retreat. How does that make any sense whatsoever?"

Jake's eyes home in on me now, suddenly sharp. Whatever I've just said, it hurt. "Let me rephrase that for you," he says, after staring at me for a moment. "I'm pretending to be Ned in a *retreat* so that no one knows Ned is in a *psychiatric institution.*"

"Oh," I say, his words piercing my skin. Suddenly the whole idea makes a lot more sense.

"Despite the lip service it gets, mental illness is still pretty socially unacceptable. Sure, it's fine to have a little issue with violence or drugs or alcohol. But live a clean life and have a small problem that you need psychiatric help for and you're labeled as mentally unstable. For life." Jake turns away now, sounding very angry indeed. His back to me, he shrugs slightly. "I guess you can believe me or not . . . but that's the truth."

I think about what Jake's just told me and come to the conclusion that—and believe me, it pains me to think it—the plan is a sound one. At least this way, Ned can get the help he needs without being hounded by the press. And if Ned is reaching out for treatment, there's no way I'd want to keep him from it with my camera—though I know plenty of others who wouldn't think twice about it.

We stand like this for a while, in silence. And I am not one of those silly blond pink princesses who carries a puppy in her purse and goes around saying "OMG," but OMG. He really is telling me the truth, I realize, focusing on the black fabric of his jacket. As I stare at it, I remember the other day, in the canoe—when I'd reached out and touched his back. I get the overwhelming sense that I want to do that again—touch him. But, this time, I don't.

"Want to fill me in on how a world-famous singer can be scared of crowds?" I ask Jake after some time. "And how no one knows about it?"

He turns back to me. "No one knows because Ned is good at hiding it. You know enough about him to know that he doesn't make that many appearances."

I nod at this, because it's true. It's all part of his allure. "Keep going," I say.

"And our father . . . he's pretty protective."

You can say that again, I think. It's also why, whenever Ned's out in public, the crowds, not to mention the paparazzi, go absolutely wild for him. There have been times when a grainy shot of Ned would have fetched more than a clear one of Sasquatch.

"So, this crowd thing. This is new to Ned?"

Jake shakes his head. "No. Old. Very old." He pauses for a second. "And it's all my fault . . ."

I'd laughed just moments before. Ned Hartnett, scared of *crowds*. But, over the next few minutes, as Jake fills me in on Ned's phobia, I don't feel like laughing again. I don't feel like laughing at all. In fact, as he tells me what happened to get Ned to this point and how it was "all his fault," as the expression on his face contorts as he returns to that place in time, I'm so taken aback by what he tells me that I almost feel like crying. And that is saying something for me. I don't cry over just anything. Or for anybody. Let alone the people I shoot on a daily basis.

Jake tells me all about how, as a child, Ned had almost been crushed to death at a ball game. Jake and Ned's father had put Jake in charge of Ned for a few minutes and had gone to speak to someone. When the ballpark's fire alarm had been set off, the crowd they were caught in surged and Ned was injured. "One minute he was there," Jake says. "I had a clear line of sight and the next, I could only see parts of him. Getting pushed and shoved. It was like he was being pulled under. Drowned."

I shake my head as I listen to Jake's vivid retelling of the event. His expressions are so raw, it's almost as if he's there again, reliving the moments he's describing to me. And as he talks, I find myself really wanting to reach out and touch him. There's a second where my hand starts to move toward his and I have to force it back. I feel my face get hot again, remembering our kiss last night. "But none of what happened is your fault," I finally tell Jake. "I mean, how old were you?"

"Almost ten. Ned was eight."

"Oh, Jake. You were a child yourself. It's not your fault something happened to Ned, it's your father's." Ugh, that Matthew Hartnett. He really is a piece of work. And obviously always was.

"It's not his fault. I didn't stay where I was told. I went

down a few rows to get a closer look at the game, and that's when everything happened."

"So you weren't with Ned?"

"I was a couple rows away. I couldn't get back to him." Jake shoves his hands in his pockets and looks out at the lake.

"That must have been awful for you." My throat closes around the words and I find them hard to get out. I'm not used to dishing out sympathy to the stars. Or their siblings. Or anyone, really.

Jake whips his head around to look at me. I think he thinks I'm joking. But then his expression softens when he sees that I'm not. "It was. I'll never forget it. Never. I couldn't hear him, but every so often I could see his face. He was looking for me. And his eyes . . . he was so scared . . ."

Silence.

"But that's good that he's getting treatment now, right?" I finally say, in the hope of making Jake feel at least a little better. "He's finally admitting he has a problem?"

Jake snorts when I say this. "Yeah, well, Ned's known all along he has a problem. It's just that our father wouldn't admit it. Until he had to."

"Had to?" I repeat, not understanding.

Jake shakes his head as if he can't believe what he's saying. "Because Ned's phobia has gone untreated, it's gotten worse. Now it's at the point where he's starting to have problems performing onstage. He was always okay with that before. He could get through a performance with that distance between himself and the crowd. But not anymore. And the public appearances that didn't involve a stage stopped a long time ago. They were the worst—when the crowd was around him. That's when he really felt out of control."

I nod, urging Jake to continue.

"But the real kicker is the cola contract."

I frown. "Cola contract?"

"The money—apparently it's the highest offer ever made to someone Ned's age. But there are a lot of public appearances involved. And I mean a *lot*. As in, worldwide. Dad is desperate for Ned to get over his phobia fast and accept the deal. Thus, the hospital. He's been there almost a week now."

"Is it working?" I ask.

Jake shrugs. "I wouldn't know. I'm too busy being Ned. So, that's it. Everything there is to know. I hope you're satisfied. You going to run off and call *Us Weekly* now?"

"No," I say, giving Jake a look, but in my head I'm thinking more along the lines of, *No, because that's not who I'm working for right now*. But of course I don't say that. Instead, we both stand for a few moments and stare at each other. And I'm guessing Jake's thinking the same thing as me: *What next?*

"So," Jake finally pipes up again. "Now that we've had our secret squirrel meeting by the lake and you know exactly what's going on here, can we get some breakfast?"

"What about the squirrel?" I'm only half listening to Jake,

a million and one thoughts running through my head as he speaks, but my ears prick up on the word "squirrel." What does he know? Has he been snooping in my room? Has he seen that shot of the squirrel I took? Does he know I sent it to Melissa? After a few seconds' freak-out, I realize Jake is giving me an odd look.

"It's a cartoon, Jo. *Secret Squirrel.* You know? The *Atom Ant/Secret Squirrel Show*? It's a sixties classic."

I shake my head. "No, I don't know. I don't watch a lot of cartoons these days. Especially ones made over forty years ago."

"Yeah, guess not. So, breakfast then?"

I shrug. "Um, sure." I push myself into action as Jake is already starting up the hill and toward the cafeteria. I have really got to learn to keep my cool. Not to mention my focus.

It's only when we've almost reached the glass frontage of the main building that Jake turns around and looks at me again. "You know, it's kind of a relief to get that out. It'll be good to have someone in here I can talk to. Someone I can trust."

★ ★ ★

I can't believe Jake Hartnett trusts me.

Me.

Me.

The very last person in here he should trust. The very

last person he should trust on the face of the planet, really. Me. A paparazzo. *Me!*

Oh, Jake. Bad call. Bad, bad call.

As I gulp down a cinnamon and raisin bagel and some orange juice in the cafeteria, I think about Melissa, who I'm supposed to be e-mailing with some shots very, very soon—most likely tonight. Melissa would kill for this information, especially the part about Matthew Hartnett putting a fake Ned in place just in case. Duping the general public *and* the media—Melissa would go insane for this story. And combine all this with the circus skills shots, like the one of Jake juggling, or spinning plates? Well, it's just all too good. If I play my cards right, she'll probably give me a bonus.

So why, then, am I looking at my watch and thinking about getting to group on time? Why am I thinking about going to group at all, when I should be off locating Rowan and getting those oh-so-important shots to Melissa earlier than this evening?

I glance across the cafeteria to stare my answer in the face.

But this time, it's not Ned Hartnett I look at. It's Jake Hartnett.

This is officially the worst assignment ever. Trust me to get stuck with a nice star I actually like. Or a nice fake star I actually like. Or . . . oh, whatever.

I should have sent those shots to Melissa last night.

When my focus was on being double-crossed and I didn't feel sorry for anyone. Especially Jake.

I sit, my juice going warm in my hands.

"Um, hey," someone says, approaching me.

I look up. "Let me guess." I sigh. "Nine to ten p.m."

Rowan winks. "You got it!"

He's about to walk away when I reach out and grab his T-shirt. "Wait!" I say.

He hesitates but then looks around him and takes a step back. The cafeteria is pretty quiet now that most people have long since finished breakfast. We're safe.

"I need, um . . . access. Just for fifteen minutes. Right now."

"Oh." Rowan glances around again. "I don't know . . ."

"One hundred bucks."

"Well, um . . . ," he says, and shrugs.

"Fine. One fifty. But that's my final offer."

★ ★ ★

Between Melissa and myself, Rowan is making some serious tips this week.

He decides to take my "final offer"—ha! I would have sprung for at least two hundred—and I run off to room 20 and log on.

Please, please, please be at home, or at least have your phone turned on. I mentally cross my fingers as I type.

ZoJo: Mannie, Mannie, Mannie. Where are you? Please be there!

Mannietheman: Jo! How's it going? How's the job?

ZoJo: Thank God. Job is . . . gah!

Mannietheman: ???

ZoJo: Hard job. Very confused. Need saving. SOS and all that.

Mannietheman: What's going on? Can I call you?

I bite my lip and think fast. No, Mannie can't call me, not with this weird cell phone business they have going on. But I am desperate to talk to him. DESPERATE. I start typing again.

ZoJo: Can't do calls, sorry. Could we try to IM again tonight? Will have more time then.

Mannietheman: Can do. Eight your time good for you?

I pause again. Nine would be better, but at nine I'll be dealing with Melissa. Still, now that I know Rowan has a price (and not as expensive as I thought), another hundred bucks or so will probably buy me the extra online time I need.

ZoJo: Eight my time is perfect. But please be waiting. BEGGING HERE. ON KNEES. GROVELING. NEED GUIDANCE.

Mannietheman: LOL. I'll be waiting.

I breathe a sigh of relief and then pray that I can make it till 8:00 p.m. unscathed.

Now, what was I doing? I look vaguely around the room. Oh, group!

I spring from my seat, slapping my laptop closed in the process, and bolt out the door.

Halfway up the hallway, I freeze, pat down my pockets, and realize I don't have any kind of camera on me.

It takes me only a split second to decide I'm not turning back.

★ ★ ★

I'm not sure what it is with group, but one of the members always manages to have some kind of mini-breakthrough each session, and it's always in the final ten minutes. I'm starting to wonder if they organize it beforehand. Maybe they even draw straws.

It can't be a boredom thing, because group is usually pretty interesting. Usually there's bickering, or someone gets weepy, or someone makes a few pointed comments. Unfortunately, today the pointed comments just happen to be directed at me.

It all starts because we're talking about the death of the nuclear family. The only person in our group who comes close to having something approximating a nuclear family is Katrina. And even then her nuclear family is sort of irradiated in the way that her dad is actually a stepdad, because her mother married him when Katrina was two, which makes her sisters half sisters.

Of course, Brad comes from a proper nuclear family. Which explains why he's messing with the heads of the messed up. Not being messed up by a modern family himself, he's a messer, not a messee.

Everyone else in the room either lives with their mom, or their dad, or a grandparent, a sibling, or two dads (that must be fun—I can barely even cope with one . . .). Some of them have stepsiblings, or half siblings, two stepdads, or are younger than all of their nieces and nephews.

Let's just say it's complicated.

Which is why I stay out of the discussion. That is, until Seth drags me in.

When there's a lull in the conversation, he leans back in his chair with a lazy smile. "So, Jo," he says. "What about you?"

I'm instantly on alert and eye him, across the circle from me. "What about me?"

"Well, you know. We're talking families and all. What about yours?"

I shrug. "There's not much to tell. Like I've said before, I live with my dad. My dad's parents died before I was born, so there's not much to tell there . . ." I trail off, everyone's eyes on me. In particular, I feel Jake watching me, just two seats away. I don't look at him.

"So what about your mom? Or your mom's parents?" He goes for the obvious question.

I sit very, very still, and try to appear calm. I need to handle this carefully and say only what I want to say. Nothing more. "Well," I start slowly, "my mom left when I was a baby. I never met her parents."

"Where'd your mom go?"

"Japan," I say quickly, then have to stop so I can word things in a way I'm comfortable with—one that doesn't give everything away. Like where she is now. "I'm half-Japanese."

"And you haven't seen her since?" Seth continues firing bulletlike questions at me. They feel like bullets, anyway.

"No." That would be impossible. I take a breath before I continue. "But that's okay. She had her reasons for leaving. I know about them. And I'm okay with it."

"Or maybe that's just what you tell yourself." Seth's eyes bore into mine.

"Hey," Jake calls out in my defense.

Brad takes the opportunity to intervene. "It's okay to talk about these things, Seth, but with respect, please."

"Sure, sorry," Seth says, fairly insincerely, I think. "Still, it would be good to know why Jo is here."

"Is that really any of your business?" I shift slightly in my chair. As for Jake, I don't look at him or thank him for sticking up for me. I've been studiously ignoring him the whole session, because every time he's in my line of sight, all I can think about is the pool.

Seth snorts. "Um, yes, it's my business. It's called 'group' for a reason, you know."

With Seth's comment, I slowly look around the circle and find that everyone is nodding at me, including Jake and even Katrina. Only Hoodie Boy avoids my gaze.

Damn. I guess it's a fair point.

"Look," I say. "I guess I'm here because I'm . . . confused." I glance around the circle again. No one looks particularly impressed with this statement, and I feel myself start to flounder. There's at least another five to ten minutes of group left, and I have no idea what to say, or how to get myself out of this.

And that's when I'm saved—not by the bell, but by something else entirely.

Today it's Hoodie Boy's turn. Just when enough time has passed so that everyone is hitting that midmorning sugar low, he stands up and actually throws his chair against the room's whiteboard with an impressive ninjalike *heeaaahhh!* It's even more impressive because I think it's the first sound any of us have ever heard out of him.

Maybe that's the retreat's secret—hitting absolute rock bottom 10:30 a.m. decaffeination to force someone to actually *do* something so we can all get out and hunt for muffins and coffee.

Brad does his usual thing, leading the troubled teen to his office, and we're all breathing sighs of relief and getting up out of our chairs when he turns back around in the doorway. "Oh, and Jo . . ."

"Yeeeees." I look over at him slowly, very, very sure I'm not going to like what I'm about to hear.

"Your individual meeting this afternoon? I'd like it if Seth can join us."

"Great! Suits me!" Seth says cheerily.

And I'm thinking maybe I don't reply fast enough, because beside me, Katrina kind of nudges my foot slightly.

"Yeah, um, okay," I answer. Because what else am I going to say?

Brad glances around the room. "We'll be assembling as per usual in the foyer in half an hour for the morning activity. You need to be wearing jeans and closed-toe shoes. I think you're going to enjoy what we have planned."

There's a collective groan, which Brad quickly mimics. "Oh, you guys. Where's your sense of adventure?" he asks, before shutting the door behind him.

As I quickly make my way back to room 20, still avoiding Jake, I agonize about what to do. After what went down in group this morning, I really want to get out of this place. I seriously consider running for it and sending Melissa her shots as soon as I hit some free Wi-Fi. Or maybe I should e-mail the shots later, or delete the shots, or try for more money, or . . .

I have no idea. In the end, I decide to wait for my chat

with Mannie and let him make up my mind for me because I've lost all capability to function rationally.

For once in my life, I'm torn. I'm never torn. I don't balk at even *taking* a shot, let alone sending one. Mostly because the stars, however much they pretend they don't want pictures of them appearing anywhere and everywhere, would be even more unhappy if there were suddenly no pictures of them on the newsstands tomorrow.

Choices are usually pretty easy in my world. Diet or regular, fries or no fries, chase the star or don't chase the star, stay put or move to a better location. But this choice impacts someone's well-being. If something happened to Ned— something along the lines of what happened to my mom—I don't think I could ever forgive myself. And while Matthew Hartnett is playing around with the media by having Jake here as a decoy, and while it might result in Ned's overcoming his issues, there's no way I want to get any more involved with this plan than I already am. If something went wrong, I wouldn't want to be a part of whatever went down. After all, there's stooping and taking sneaky shots, and then there's diving deep into the primordial swamp.

Still, I have to do something, and there must be a way to get out of all this with my paycheck and dreams of photography school intact. So, even though I don't feel like doing it, I decide to take my fauxPod with me this morning, see if I can get a few decent shots, and take it from there. Think of it as insurance.

"Jo?" I look up from my seat on the bed to see Katrina standing above me. "It's time to go."

"Oh, right," I say, standing up.

"Come on, or we'll be late."

We make our way out to the foyer, where the rest of the group is waiting.

"Ah, there they are." Brad ticks two final names off on his clipboard. "I hope you're all ready to get dirty!"

Beside me, I can feel Katrina stiffen. I guess ballerinas aren't really into getting dirt under their fingernails.

Brad ends up leading us outside and down toward the woods. As we get closer, it's obvious that there's something going on in there. Through the trees, we catch glimpses of large orange objects. In a clearing, there's a man and two women waiting for us, along with what looks like two racks of black vests and other equipment lying on the ground on huge sheets.

"Hi," the guy greets our group when we reach him. "I'm Michael. I'm thinking a couple of you will have already guessed what we're up to today."

"Paintball?" someone answers from the back of the group.

"Close," Michael replies. "Because of the area we're playing in and the fact that we can't make too much mess in there for environmental reasons, we're going to be playing a kind of modified version of paintball called V-ball." Michael goes on to explain the equipment and how the game works. I try not to laugh as I remember this game I had on the back of my bedroom door as a kid: a large Velcro dartboard. I kept the balls in a container on my bedside table and would occasionally hurl them at the dartboard when I could be bothered. It's sounding like V-ball is pretty much like that, except you turn it into a moving Velcro dartboard and instead of throwing the little balls, everyone's given a gun with a hundred of the things loaded in it and sent off to run around and shoot each other like idiots.

Not exactly my weapon of choice, but then neither is a fauxPod.

We all get loaded up in vests, armbands, leg bands, and full face masks and are then each handed a gun complete with tiny colored Velcro balls.

"I never thought I'd call ammunition cute, but you've got to admit . . ." I nudge Katrina with my free arm.

She laughs. "They actually are pretty cute. Maybe we should just sit around and string them or something. Make V-ball necklaces."

Speaking of cute, I am extremely aware of someone's presence behind me. I'm sure Jake's watching—staring at my back, if that hot spot between my shoulder blades is any-thing to go by. I move slightly to one side as Michael explains how to fire our guns and gets each of us to step forward and fire at a large Velcro target.

When it's my turn, I step forward and fire.

"Bull's-eye! Wow, that's great." Michael nods. "You've got a good eye."

And I'm getting paid for it, I feel like saying. Though the way I'm going, refusing to send Melissa my shots, I may not have been paid anything at all. I really should check on that.

"Okay," Michael continues, when we've all fired at the target. "The first game we're going to play today is a free-for-all called Elimination. This means you'll be playing for yourself, rather than as a team." He gestures toward the woods before continuing. "As you can see, we've roped off a specific playing field and the large blow-up orange structures give you some coverage. What you're looking to do is eliminate everyone else by shooting them, until you're the last person standing. You'll get a few minutes to look around now, then a warning bell, then there's thirty seconds until we begin play, when another bell will sound again to let you know it's all on. Good luck, troops!"

Everyone else starts forward into the woods, but Katrina stands still. "That's it? That's all the training we get?"

"Oh, don't be such a prima donna!" I give her a wink, which I then realize she can't see under my mask, so I grab her arm and start dragging her into the woods with me. "I'm sure the ballet world was way more cutthroat than this will be."

"Huh. True." Katrina's mask nods at me.

"Well then, let's go shoot some people. And dibs on me shooting Seth first. If I get lucky, he might not be able to make it to our session this afternoon."

chapter 14

Okay, so I am loving V-ball. A little too much, actually, I'm thinking as I run, throw myself behind another one of the orange blow-up structures and *boom, boom, boom, boom, boom* take out someone or other (it's kind of hard to tell with these masks on). Whoever it is swears, then trudges off the playing field, his or her front littered with little pink balls.

So undignified.

I laugh and can't help myself . . . *thwack!* I let another one fly and hit them square in the back.

"Hey!" They turn around, giving me a rude gesture, and I can't help but laugh again.

Like I said, I'm loving this fantastic distraction they call V-ball just a little too much. It's been great not to think about

Jake for ten minutes, for a start. Though I do wonder what Brad would make of this. I've probably got a whole lot of repressed anger going on or something.

A long silence follows, in which I have time to slowly look around at my surroundings and realize there can't be that many people left in the game. Then I hear something—footsteps, the snapping of a twig—not close, but close enough to be worried.

More silence.

And then *thwack, thwack, thwack* and, "Oh, I hate you, whoever you are!" Which is so Katrina. She's done amazingly well to make it this far when she wasn't even into the game to begin with. I must have been right, after all, about ballet being cutthroat.

I'm just waiting for the silence to kick in again, but it doesn't. Instead, I suddenly hear someone running very close to me and I can't tell which side of the structure they're going to come in on, or where I should shoot. I try to scramble out of my crouching position and into more of a starter's position in case I need to run, but by then it's too late . . .

Crash!

Someone comes barreling in from the side of the structure I'm hiding behind and tackles me to the ground. I don't think they'd realized I was there at all.

I wind up crushed beneath them, gasping for breath as their weight bears down on my lungs.

"Hey, are you okay?" The person rolls off me as I take a

noisy, shuddery breath. They ditch their gun and reach forward to pull my mask off my face. "Jo? Are you okay? Breathe!"

I take another raspy breath, then force myself to take a slower, longer one. I've been winded before—the worst thing you can do is lie there gasping for breath like a fish out of water. It just prolongs the agony. After yet another long breath, I start to think I might live. "How much do you *weigh*?" I finally say, with a cough.

My assailant strips off his own mask. It's Jake. Of course. "Sorry," he says. "I'm trying to cut back on the bacon bits."

We stare at each other for a moment or two until I realize the situation we're in—alone, just like we'd been the other night. And then I become suddenly breathless again. "So, is this where you shoot me?" I finally ask him.

"I sort of had other ideas," he says, moving forward, and my heart really starts pounding. He *is* going to kiss me again.

But he doesn't. When he's as near to me as he can be, his green eyes locked onto mine, Jake takes one of the pink Velcro V-balls and balances it on the bridge of my nose. "Huh," he says, inspecting it. "Cute!" He gives me a look that is very not-what-you-thought-I-was-going-to-do-was-it?

For a second or two, I'm thrown. But that's the beauty of the element of surprise. It's a game two can play, and I've never been a girl who hangs around and waits for things she can have right now. So I decide to take what I want. I push myself up on one elbow and before Jake can say anything else, my lips are against his once more, exactly how I've wanted them to be ever since they parted last night. And I didn't think a kiss could be any better than the one we'd already shared, but I was wrong. This one's better. At that thought, I start to smile.

"What's so funny?" Jake pulls back an inch, one eyebrow raised. But then I think he realizes I'm not poking fun at him and he grins back at me. "I guess it's not the most romantic of times and places, is it?" he picks two Velcro balls out of my hair and flicks them aside.

I laugh. "It's a step up from the chlorinated pool." I sit all the way up and note that I'm still holding my gun in my right hand. I glance at it and then shrug, dropping it. I can hardly shoot him now that I've kissed him, can I?

"I think we're the last two left." Jake moves in beside me. "Want to keep them guessing?"

"Sure, why not?" I could hang out here all day with Jake. Not a problem.

Jake is quiet for a moment or two as we sit side by side, then he turns to look at me. "I wanted to tell you—I got to speak to Ned last night. Brad arranged it for me."

When he says this, I get the sudden urge to jump up and kiss him again. Because I really don't think I want to hear what he has to say about Ned or be reminded of what I'm doing here yet again. And I'd almost forgotten about my fauxPod tucked inside my vest, but now I feel its weight, solid against my chest. "Really?" I say slowly. "How's he doing?"

Jake nods, looking kind of relieved. "He sounded pretty good. Upbeat. He said the treatment was working really well for him, that he felt better just for being there, doing something about it."

"Wow, that's great!" I say. And I do mean it. After all, it's not like I wish terrible things on Ned. I don't want him to lead some miserable life where he can't go out and perform in front of his fans. I also just don't want him to unintentionally make my life miserable, either. Though I'm sure Melissa will need no help in that regard if I don't produce some shots. And soon.

Don't think about it, Jo. Just don't think about it.

"What's great is that I was able to talk to you about it. I was going slightly crazy in here—" He starts to move in closer to me once more when someone shouts, interrupting the moment.

"Only two people left!" Brad's voice rings out through the woods.

On hearing Brad, we both pull back from each other.

I gulp. "So, what's the plan? I shoot you? You shoot me?" *We stay here forever and kiss every so often?* (I'll take what's behind door number three.)

Jake grins. "Neither. I've got a better idea."

★ ★ ★

"Okay, ready?" Jake looks at me from the opposite end of the structure we're still hidden behind, or at least I think he looks at me from behind his mask. He looks in my direction, anyway.

I nod back at him.

"One . . . two . . . three."

On the count of three, we both jump up from our opposite ends and let each other have it. We empty about half our cartridges onto each other's front, then I jump around and Jake empties his other half onto my back, and then I do the same to him when he's finished V-balling me.

When we're both done, Jake takes a step in, grabs my hand, and lifts it high in the air in a "we are the V-balling champions" salute.

That done, we both check each other out and laugh. Jake's front and back are completely covered in sticky little pink balls, while I'm covered in yellow ones. It's an interesting look.

Michael waves us in and we make our way over to the other side of the clearing, where the group is waiting. I'm sad to leave the game behind. For just a few minutes, I'd managed to forget everything else that's going on. For that time, Jake and I were nothing more than a guy and a girl. As I stroll back over to the group, I let myself wonder for a moment or two whether that's what life's like on the outside. Where normal people have normal relationships. I can't remember.

Michael gives us a debriefing and talks about the next

game we'll be playing as everyone helps pick balls off Jake and me and we reload our cartridges. When I'm finally done, Katrina yanks me over to one side.

"What were you doing back there?" she whispers.

"Huh?"

"You and Ned. What were you doing? You were behind that blow-up for*ever*."

"No, we weren't," I say quickly.

"Yes, you were! What were you doing?"

I pause for only a second. "Strategizing? It really wasn't that long, Katrina. What did you think we were doing?"

She gives me a funny look. As, I've already noticed, does Brad, and he has been ever since Jake and I rejoined the group.

But it's true, what I've just told Katrina. The time Jake and I spent behind that blow-up? It wasn't that long. Unfortunately, however, it was just long enough for me to feel terrible for Ned all over again. Just long enough to realize I'm not going to be taking any shots this morning, either. And just long enough to know that my whole plan to ignore Jake was something that was never going to happen in this lifetime.

I check my watch around five million times as the rest of the day slowly passes by. Eight hours and twenty-five minutes till I get to IM Mannie. Seven hours and forty-two minutes till I get to IM Mannie. Seven hours and forty-one minutes and fifty-three seconds till I get to IM Mannie.

Not that I'm counting or anything.

"So, family phone call night tonight." Katrina places her knife and fork together, having finished her lunch at exactly seven hours and twenty-eight minutes till I get to IM Mannie and hopefully get some perspective on this whole situation. "Who are you calling, Ned?" she asks, and looks across the table at him.

Jake shrugs, his mouth full of (you guessed it) bacon bits. I guess he wasn't serious about slowing down on those things. It takes him a second or two to swallow. "My dad, I guess. No one exciting, that's for sure. You?"

Katrina grins. "I'm in luck. I'll probably get one of my sisters. I think my mom and dad are out at a fund-raiser tonight. If it's Sara, we'll talk about her boyfriend, because that's all Sara talks about. If it's Emily, we'll talk about swimming, because that's all Emily talks about. Either is fine by me, because I won't have to talk about me, or ballet, or me and ballet, or even ballet and me for one boring second. What about you, Jo?"

"My cousin Wendy, probably. Just to check in." Funnily enough, I forget to add that I'll also be putting in a call to the boss from hell.

Until that time, however, I have another kind of hell to contend with and here he comes now. "Seth," I say. A hush falls over our table as he approaches.

"It's time," he tells me.

I abandon the rest of my salad, push back my chair, and make my way out of the cafeteria with Seth by my side. "You're really looking forward to this, aren't you?" I give him a quick, sideways glance as we walk. What a freak.

He shrugs slightly. "I've got quite a chunk of change riding on this."

I stop in my tracks. "Are you serious? Is that what this is about? Money?"

"Oh, come on, Jo. It's not just about that. You can't expect to just come to a place like this and get away with being 'confused,' while everyone else spills their guts. Can you?" Seth doesn't stop alongside me, but continues walking up the corridor that leads to Brad's office.

I watch him go but don't answer him. Because the truth is, that's exactly what I'd been hoping to do. And now I've been called on it.

"Jo, Seth." Brad opens his door for us after Seth knocks on it eagerly. "Good to see you. Come in."

"After you," Seth motions to me.

"You really can't wait, can you?" I roll my eyes as I pass by. I'm hoping this will be a nice, friendly chat about being "respectful" in group. Maybe even a nice, friendly, *quick* chat about being "respectful" in group, and then off for some free time.

"Take a seat." Brad goes to sit behind his desk, and Seth and I take the two chairs on the opposite side. When he's settled in his seat, Brad clasps his hands together and watches us, a half smile on his face. I think it's supposed to be a kindly smile, but somehow it only reminds me of the wolf in Little Red Riding Hood. Really, he wants to tear us to shreds and see what's making us tick.

"So, you wanted to see us both?" I begin. May as well get this over and done with. The faster the better.

"Yes, I did," Brad says. "That was a very interesting discussion we had going on in group today, don't you think?"

"You mean the discussion about nuclear families or the interrogation Seth gave me afterward?" I try a half smile on for size.

"Interrogation?" Seth laughs at my choice of words. "Hardly."

"Oh, it gets worse? Will you pull out the red-hot pokers tomorrow, or is water torture more your thing?"

Brad waits to intervene until after we've both finished bickering. "I should say I wasn't completely comfortable with the tone we had going on in group today, but I do see Seth's point, Jo."

"Remind me what it was again?" I say, stalling, knowing full well what Seth's been getting at.

"Seth's point was that you can't expect to get much out of group without being willing to fully participate. It's unfair to the others and it's unfair to you, too."

Hmmm. I don't exactly see how it's unfair to me, considering I'm getting to keep my mouth closed like I want to, but

I decide to let this one go, rather than argue the point. "Okay," I agree, just to keep the peace. "I'll think about that. Maybe I'll be able to share a bit more tomorrow." That is, after I've had time to make something up that everyone will believe and that I can live with.

"That's great, Jo." Brad beams. "I'll look forward to that."

"Me, too," I tell him, lying wholeheartedly. "So, is that all?" I ask him.

"I think we've covered everything nicely," he tells me. "I just wanted to make sure we're on the same page. Seth? Do you have anything to add?"

But when I turn my head to look at Seth, I see that he doesn't seem to think we've covered everything nicely or that we're on the same page at all. He does, however, look like he might have a lot of things to add.

"That's it?" Seth glances from Brad to me, a look of incredulity plastered all over his face. "That's it? You're going to let her get away with this?" He sits forward in his seat, edging closer to Brad's desk.

"Now, Seth." Brad straightens in his chair.

I laugh a fake laugh. "What did you expect, Seth? That I was going to come in here and open up to you? Why should I? It's not like you give a damn about me. It's not like you're asking because you care—you're asking because you've got a pool going on whatever my issues are!"

"Seth." Brad's eyes darken as they home in on him. "Is that true?"

"No," Seth barks.

Pffft, is my only response. What a liar.

Seth swivels in his seat to face me, looking angrier than I've ever seen him look before (which is saying something). "Do you know how annoying it is to have to sit there in group, or go to activities like the circus skills thing, with someone who isn't willing to put it all out there?"

I stare at his face, watching it get redder by the second.

"It's pretty unbearable to have everyone else share their innermost thoughts and embarrass themselves with, you know, emotion and snot bubbles and stuff, while you listen in and then make some throwaway comment or say nothing at all."

I'd love to pick up on the snot bubble but feel it would be unnecessarily cruel. "What's your issue with me?" I shake my head at him. "Why don't you pick on Hoodie Boy? He never says anything!"

"You mean Ethan," Brad says, and both Seth and I turn to look at him for a second, not sure what he's talking about. Then I realize that Hoodie Boy has a name. Well, there you go.

"Sure, him. Ethan." I turn back again and Seth does the same.

But Seth just rolls his eyes at the mention of Ethan. "Well, duh. Hoodie Boy's problem *is* not talking. Pretty obvious, that one."

"You mean Ethan," Brad pipes up again.

Seth and I both ignore him this time.

I sigh. "So what? I'm annoying. Well, deal with it, Seth. Lots of people on this earth are annoying. But the truth is, I don't owe you anything. I don't know you and you don't know me. You're just some random guy at some random place to me. I don't want to know you. I don't want to know about your problems. And I don't want you to know about mine, either." I wish I *had* brought up the snot bubble now.

"Aha!" Seth points a finger at me. "So you admit there is a problem?"

I don't know what it is about this small statement, but it makes something inside me snap. I stand up, furious now. I notice my hands are shaking slightly, which for me is a scary thing. My hands *never* shake. Ever. I'd been about to simply stomp out of the room, but seeing my hands quiver makes me even angrier, if that's possible. At myself, mostly, for letting Seth and this place get to me. I should have been more professional and taken the shots I needed and gotten out in twenty-four hours tops. I should have known better. I shouldn't have gotten involved. And now I'm paying for it by caring about Jake and by having to play games with idiots like Seth.

"You don't get it, do you?" I forcefully push my chair away. "Of course there's a problem. There's always a problem. Your brother died, Seth. That's a terrible thing, and I'm not lying when I say I'm truly sorry that it happened to him, to you, and to your family. But you know something?

Everyone here's got a dead brother in one way or another. We've all got a career that's not going to happen, like Katrina, or an overbearing father, like Ned, or can't talk to people, like Ethan, or—" I stop myself here, before I regret saying anything more. I already regret enough of what I've let spill from my mouth. "Anyway, we're all the same. Just in different ways."

Before I can dig myself in further, I make for the door. I grasp the handle and pull it open firmly, almost knocking myself out in the process. I'm halfway through the doorway when Brad's words ring out, making me pause.

"And what have you got, Jo?"

I swivel around.

"I've got a mother who committed suicide right after she had me." I look Seth straight in the eye. "Hope you guessed right on that one."

chapter 15

I run down the hall toward room 20, not stopping when I pass a bunch of people, one of whom calls out my name.

I'm praying Katrina isn't in our room, and when I get back there, I'm lucky—she's not. I slam the door shut behind me and go straight over to my backpack, where I fish out my fauxPod from the secret compartment I've made for it in the lining. Then I stand there, still and silent, and stare at it. At this stupid, useless device that's gotten me into this mess. And I want to slam it into the floor. I want to slam it so hard it will never take another fauxShot, ever.

For a good thirty seconds or so, I hold it tightly in my hand, my fingernails digging into the plastic casing surrounding it, its life in the balance. I want to destroy it so badly, I really do. But I also know I'm not going to. The faux-Pod might have gotten me into this mess, but it's also the only thing that can get me out of this messy life of mine for good—and into photography school.

In the end, I do throw it. Hard. But only onto my bed. It bounces off the duvet and then falls to the floor. As it does, I instantly regret what I've done and jump into action, racing over. I fall to my knees and pick it up, cradling it, checking to see if it's okay.

It's fine. But I'm not. How pathetic am I? I couldn't have destroyed it even if I'd wanted to; I don't have the guts. And it's with this realization that I start crying. I couldn't even say what for—because I'm way too attached to a piece of tech-nology, because I'm not brave enough to give up a job I don't truly love, because I'm stuck deceiving people I like for nothing more than money, because I had a mother I'll never be able to know. Maybe all of those things.

After I don't know how long, there's a knock on the door.

"Come in," I say with a shrug, leaning back against my bed. I don't have the energy to keep out whoever it is.

"Jo?" a voice says quietly.

Without even turning around, I know it's Jake. I realize then that he was the one who'd called out to me in the cor-ridor.

"I'm down here." I hold up one hand.

"Can I come in?"

"Sure, why not. Join the party." I don't even bother to hide my fauxPod. I just don't care anymore.

Jake comes over to stand in between the two beds, where I'm sitting on the floor, my knees pulled up. "You okay?" he sinks down to my level.

I can only sniff.

"Seth's outside. I think he feels pretty bad. He wants to talk to you."

"I think Seth's done enough talking for one day."

Jake sits down next to me on the floor. "I know he's a pain, but he's also pretty messed up, Jo. His brother died because they swapped their usual seats in the car the day of the accident. And he's having a hard time dealing with that. I mean, it doesn't excuse what he says or does, but it might help you understand why."

I sniff again. It's about all I'm capable of right now.

"He told me. About your mom. I'm sorry, Jo. That must be really hard for you." Jake reaches out and touches me on the arm.

I flinch and pull away. I don't deserve his kindness. "She died when I was only a few months old. She took her own life, Jake. She had postpartum depression, but it was more than that—it was all sort of combined with her having been bipolar for a long time. Her parents hadn't wanted to know, and she'd gotten treatment late and . . ." I sigh because it's a long, involved, sad story. My dad's told me about my mom's past, but I'm sure there's a lot he left out.

"My dad thought she was doing okay after I was born, and she was seeing a psychiatrist, just to make sure. But she wasn't okay. Anyway, what you told me this morning—about Ned—I get why you don't want people to know he's in a psychiatric institution. It's not about being ashamed or anything like that. The media would just be all over him, and it would make it even harder to get the help he needs. People don't understand." I don't look at Jake. Or can't. One or the other.

"That's a terrible thing to have happen to you," Jake says, after a while. "It doesn't get much worse than that, Jo."

I shrug by way of reply. "It is what it is." I use my dad's line.

"Don't say that." Jake reaches out once more and grabs onto my forearm, making me turn toward him. "Don't ever say that again."

Now I do meet his eyes, which are filled with concern. "Why not?"

"Because I know you don't mean it. What happened to your mom—and to you—it can't be brushed off in five insignificant words."

We sit in silence for a few more minutes and I let Jake hug me to his side. After a while, he asks if Seth can come in. I say yes, mainly because I'm going to have to talk to him at some point and it may as well be now.

When Jake leaves and Seth enters the room, he closes the door behind him and then kind of hovers. "Sit down, Seth, you're making me nervous," I finally say with a sigh.

He does what he's told and comes over, sitting on the edge of the bed. I swivel around to look at him. For a moment or two, we simply stare at each other. "Sorry," he says, eventually. "About before."

I shrug. "It's okay. We're all messed up in our own special way."

Seth nods. "I guess it's like Brad says: the world would be a boring place if we were all the same."

Sounds like Brad. "And he'd be out of a job," I say pointedly. The tension seems to loosen as both Seth and I have a good laugh at this, because it's so true. But when the laughter dies down again, I realize Seth's pain is so constant and underlying, I could see it even when he was laughing, supposedly enjoying himself. "You'll be okay, Seth," I tell him. "You'll be different after this, but you'll be okay."

"Yeah," he says after a long pause, the fingers of one hand clutching at the comforter of the bed he's sitting on. "I'm looking forward to okay. Okay looks like a good place to be from where I am right now."

Seth doesn't stay for much longer, but it's enough for us to make our peace. And it's not like we'll ever be best friends, but I know I'll want to find out how he fares over the next few years. I really do think he'll be all right. He was telling the truth in Brad's office, I see that now—he didn't want to know about my problems to win any bet. He wanted to know because it genuinely pained him to have to sit there in group and share when someone else wasn't. Which, I hate to admit, makes a lot of sense. If I were him, I wouldn't want to, either.

★ ★ ★

That afternoon, we have a choice of activities, and one of them is picnic blankets and reading books on the lawn. Jake, Katrina, and I sign ourselves up, but I make them promise that there will be no talking. I'm sick of talking.

They are true to their word and we have the best afternoon rolling around on our picnic blankets, half in the shade, half in the sun. I actively make myself not think about anything that's gone on between Jake and me (I've got to stop before my brain implodes), and we don't talk unless it's to ask to pass the snacks or to read aloud something funny. There's a choice of books (no magazines allowed, which is more than fine by me), and I try some Dickens, whom I've never read before. It's actually not too bad—pretty crazy stuff. I could totally see him writing something about the world of the paparazzi. You know, if he wasn't already dead and everything.

My fauxPod and fauxglasses remain in my bag, in room 20. And I barely give them a passing thought.

The funny thing is, I didn't know I could have a great time without a camera in my hand. But honestly, it's one of the best times I've had in ages.

★ ★ ★

Brad reminds us before dinner that it's family phone call night tonight. I check the bulletin board—7:20 p.m. is my allotted time.

At precisely 7:18 p.m. I go out to reception, grab the phone, and sign for my call. Since Katrina's in the lounge, I take it into our bedroom and call Wendy's number, hoping that she'll be home. I don't think she's flying out again for another day or two, so there's a good chance she will be.

"Hello?"

"Wendy, hi. It's me, Jo." I pull out the white chair tucked under the desk and sit down.

"Hey, Jo! How's the sanctuary? Elephants giving you any trouble?"

I groan. Melissa could easily be described as a stamping elephant right now. "It's not too bad," I tell Wendy, then think of the next phone call coming up. The one I really should make—to Melissa herself. "Yet."

"Seriously, though, everything okay?" Wendy tries again.

"Yeah, I'm okay. Perfectly . . . safe." I'm not going to say everything's been working out fantastically, because it really hasn't. But I am safe. That's something.

Well, I'm safe for the next few minutes, anyway. "Thanks for your messages and everything. Sorry I haven't been able to get back to you. Communication with the outside world here is kind of . . . limited."

"Sounds like fun."

"Oh yeah," I say and laugh a fake laugh. "We're all

having a ball. Look, there's not much time, but could you do me a quick favor while I've got you on the phone?"

"Sure."

"Could you check out my bank account details? I want to see if any money's been transferred into it yet. Because thinking I might have been paid is pretty much the only thing getting me through one minute to the next in here." I could access this information myself from room 20, given a little online time, but I'm getting jumpier by the minute—and I'm sure they monitor any and all time spent on the Internet. Anyway, even if I was paid, it's very possible I'll have to give the money back, but I want to check that Melissa's at least kept her end of the bargain so far—you never know with her.

"Of course. Just hang on."

I hear Wendy starting up her computer, then typing. "Okay," she says, and I spend the next couple of minutes directing her on how to get into my online bank account. When she's finally into the account itself, she starts reading things out to me. The first few transactions are debits. Mostly restaurants. "Geez, Jo, you really should start eating in more often," she tells me. "Buy some groceries here and there."

"Yes, dear, wise cousin. Like you do."

"Hey, I buy groceries!"

"That go bad every time you leave the country."

"Well, at least I buy them!"

"Wendy! I don't have very long. Can we argue about my grocery shopping habits when I get back to LA?"

"Okay, sorry. Oh, hang on. Here you go. Holy cow! Yes, you got paid. Yesterday morning. What is this job, anyway? That's a lot of money, even for you, Little Miss Richie. I hope you really are safe there . . ."

"I'm fine," I insist, then I get Wendy to read out the exact amount, which I jot down. "And can you read me the invoice number, too?"

"Hmmm," Wendy says. "There's no number, but the payment seems to have originated from one ML Entertainment."

"ML Entertainment? That can't be right." The payment amount is correct for what I agreed on with Melissa, but I should have an invoice number from her paper, like I always do. Not something from ML Entertainment, whoever they are. Though the business name does ring a bell for some reason. "And that's all it says? No invoice number? Nothing else?"

"Nope, that's it. Just the payment amount and ML Entertainment."

"Weird." I get her to run through any and all payments in and out of my account from the day before I left for Boston until now, but there's no way around it—that money is the money Melissa agreed to pay me. So why is it coming from a company called ML Entertainment? It just doesn't make sense.

"Okay, thanks, Wendy. I'll check in again soon."

"You do that. I'm off for London tomorrow, but you've got my cell. You know you can always get me."

"I know. Thanks again. I mean it. See you!" I say, and hang up.

I look at the phone in my hand for a second or two and think about calling Melissa, but my fingers end up dialing Mannie's cell instead, praying I'll get away with one extra call.

For some reason, I do. The person manning the desk must not be paying very close attention. "Hey, Mannie, it's Jo!" I say when he picks up.

"Jo! I'm just about home. Can be with you in a few minutes. Not bailing on our chat, are you?"

"Not likely." I shake my head. "Things are only going from bad to worse here. I just wanted to check you weren't held up. And while you're here, can you tell me something? ML Entertainment. Why do I know that name?"

There's a long silence on the end of the line.

"Mannie?" I finally say. "Are you still there?"

"No way," are his words when he finally speaks. "Big money. Ned Hartnett fainting the other night. ML Entertainment. You're on the tail of Ned Hartnett, aren't you?"

"What?" I say. "How'd you guess that?"

Mannie cracks up.

"What?" I say, frowning. "What's so funny?"

"Jo, don't you know your BFF's middle name?"

"Huh?" I have no idea what he's talking about.

"It's Luke."

"Luke? Who's Luke?"

"No one. Like I said, it's your BFF's *middle* name. Matthew *Luke* Hartnett. ML Entertainment. Now do you get it?"

chapter 16

"Jo? Jo? Are you there?"

"Talk soon," I say absentmindedly, giving Mannie maybe .2 percent of my attention. I take the phone from my ear and end the call, the other 99.8 percent trying to connect the thoughts that are zinging around in my brain, like crazy, superbouncy tiny V-balls.

Okay, slow down, V-balls. Slow down.

I take a deep breath and try to be logical about this. I try to catch and line up the crazy, superbouncy tiny V-balls into some kind of order. I stare at the white table before me and work out what I know.

Okay, so here it is:

1. MELISSA HIRED ME FOR THIS JOB, BUT
   MATTHEW (LUKE!) HARTNETT IS PAYING ME;

2. MATTHEW HARTNETT HAS PLANTED JAKE AT
   THE RETREAT TO LOOK LIKE NED'S HERE;

3. MATTHEW HARTNETT IS PAYING ME TO TAKE
   SHOTS OF JAKE BEING NED AND TO GIVE
   THEM TO MELISSA, APPARENTLY SO PEOPLE
   WILL KNOW HE'S HERE; AND

4. MATTHEW HARTNETT WANTS THE SHOTS TO
   LOOK AS IF HE'S NOT BEHIND ANY OF THIS
   AND THAT "NED" IS BEING EXPOSED, PAP-
   STYLE, IN MELISSA'S PAPER.

Now, math has never been my best subject, but even I can see that adding $1 + 2 + 3 + 4$ in this situation = Matthew Hartnett is using me. Via Melissa and Jake.

I clench the phone in my hand as, suddenly, a whole lot of things make a whole lot of sense. No wonder Melissa wasn't concerned about Ned's so-called privacy. His privacy was hardly going to be breached, considering Matthew Hart-nett, his very own father-manager, would be signing off on all the photos himself.

That Matthew Hartnett. I should have known he would never have been doing this for the right reasons. As if he would have planted Jake here "just in case." He's planted Jake here "just in case" and then made very sure that he spun a decent amount of publicity out of it. "Class clown Ned takes time out!" I can just see his grin as he picks up his morning paper and sees the not-exactly-flattering shots of Jake that I took at the circus skills workshop, complete with a little story to follow about how Ned is "getting some rest." I mean, as if this was ever going to be about Ned receiving the treatment he needs for the right reasons. Oh no. It was all about Matthew Hartnett, his precious cola contract and Ned still receiving a whole heap of publicity while he was out of the spotlight for a couple of weeks. And wouldn't he have loved those V-ball shots? Or shots of "Ned" canoeing on the lake?

Yeah? Well, guess what. Just like Melissa, he's not getting them.

I knew taking this job was a bad idea. I knew there had to be more to it. And there is—so much more. I know I only took it because I wanted the money so badly for school. Because, one day, I knew I'd need to get out and get on with what I really wanted to do. Well, that time has come a bit earlier than I thought. Because that's it for me.

I'm out.

Out of papping, I mean. For good. No more Zo Jo.

I've had enough. I'd rather work split shifts at some fast food place, or cover kids parties, or shoot pet portraits than do a job like this again—do any papping job again, actually. And it's not just what's happened with Jake and Ned. It's everything. All of it. I'm sick of it. Sick of being sworn at, spit at, kicked, used, falling asleep at my desk and being hounded by Ms. Forman.

I'm beaten. It's over. I'd take that Kiddifoto job at the mall before I'd chase another star again.

I push my chair back from the desk with such force that I almost tip over backward. When I right myself, adrenaline pumping through my body, I'm still clutching the phone. I look around me. For a second, I think about storming out and finding Jake, grabbing him and then . . . what? Oh, I don't know. I don't know what to do with Jake anymore—yell at him, take shots of him, kiss him.

But then something makes me pause. I think back quickly over all our interactions—I think about the circus skills workshop, the talk about what we'd change, canoeing, the pen incident with Seth, our kiss in the pool, our talk by the lake, V-ball . . . wait! Did he know? Did he know who I was? Who I am?

I keep flicking through my memories like pages in a photo album, thinking, analyzing. Did he know? Could he possibly know?

Finally, I stop. No. I don't think he does.

But that doesn't mean he isn't aware there's someone here taking shots of him—that he isn't in on Matthew Hartnett's plan. He was pretty jumpy when it came to that pen and Seth. The thought makes my blood boil.

But what does it matter? I've got to stop thinking about Jake and start thinking about me.

Right now what matters is getting out of here.

And fast.

But first—Mannie.

★ ★ ★

I take my laptop into the bathroom, lock the door, and turn the shower on so I'll have some privacy. It doesn't take long for Mannie to send me a message.

> **Mannietheman:** Jo? You there?
>
> **ZoJo:** Here!
>
> **Mannietheman:** You all right? You're weirding me out.
>
> **ZoJo:** I'm weirding me out. Never been so confused in my life.
>
> **Mannietheman:** What's going on?
>
> **ZoJo:** Get comfy. Long story coming your way.

And it is a long story. It's a good thing we're not on Twitter because I need a lot more than 140 characters per Tweet to tell this tale. When I'm done, there's a pause from Mannie's end, then . . .

> **Mannietheman:** Wow! That's some story. And some trippy job. Matthew Hartnett—he'll get publicity any way, anyhow, huh?

ZoJo: Even at the expense of his own kids. He makes me sick.

Mannietheman: Look, none of that matters now. It's all in the past. What you need is a plan for the future.

ZoJo: Tell me about it. But I'm all planned out. Can't get a decent grip on this.

Mannietheman: You're in too deep.

ZoJo: You can say that again. I've gotten to know Jake and now he's a person, not a target. I don't think he knows what's really going on.

Mannietheman: He doesn't know you're a pap?

ZoJo: No. Don't think so.

Mannietheman: Think he knows what his dad is really up to?

ZoJo: No. And don't think he's lying to me, either.

Mannietheman: That's heavy. Give me a minute to think . . .

In the intermission, I change positions from my uncomfortable seat on the toilet to another uncomfortable position sitting on the bathroom's hard gray tiles, my back against the wall. Finally, I can't wait any longer.

ZoJo: If it were you in my position? Gut reaction?

Mannietheman: Okay. Gut reaction? I'd get out. I'd keep the shots I had and scram. Try to pull together a plan in LA.

Instantly, I know he's right. And as I think about the implications, I nod slowly as I stare at my computer screen.

ZoJo: You're right. So right. I'm already freezing up on taking shots as it is. No point in staying.

Mannietheman: Jo . . . I know you're angry, but don't delete the shots you've got. Half of what we're going on here is guesswork, yeah?

ZoJo: True. I hear you.

Mannietheman: I know you like this Jake guy, but try to keep your emotions out of it for now. Cover all your bases. Have you spoken to your dad?

ZoJo: My dad?

Mannietheman: He'd have some good advice on this.

ZoJo: Haven't spoken to him. It would give him too much satisfaction. Also, he'll probably disown me when I tell him I'm getting out.

Mannietheman: What? For real? Forever?

ZoJo: Have had enough.

Mannietheman: That's huge. But not true about your dad. You know that.

ZoJo: Do I? Anyway, don't want to argue about this now. Appreciate your advice.

Mannietheman: No problem. Good luck and promise you'll meet me for lunch Thursday when we're both back in LA. I want to see how this all pans out . . .

chapter 17

"Jo? What's going on?" Katrina enters the room just as I'm shoving my toiletries on top of my bag and zipping it up. "What are you doing?"

"Quick," I say to her, "give me your phone number and e-mail address. Just write them down. On anything. I can't stop. I've got to go." I'd exited the bathroom, toiletries in hand, laptop under my arm, and simply started throwing things into my bag.

Katrina looks confused at my request but goes over to the desk and does what I've asked. "I don't understand," she says as she writes. "Why are you leaving?"

"It's nothing about here. It's external. I've got to go home."

She walks over and hands me the piece of paper, her face reading several different expressions at once—sadness, confusion, excitement. "Is everyone okay? Are you okay?"

I nod. "Everyone's fine. Including me. It's just . . . a work thing. I'll explain later, okay?"

"Okay," Katrina replies after a moment or two.

I take a step over and give her a quick hug. Or I give her waist a hug, anyway, considering our height difference. "Don't look like that. Life continues on the outside, remember? In five minutes you'll be out of here and we'll be in touch."

"I know," Katrina says.

"Just do me one favor," I say as I grab my bag from the bed, place it on the floor, and then swing on my backpack.

"Sure. What is it?" Katrina answers.

"If anyone asks where I am, just say you're not sure, but that you've seen me around. That's not exactly lying, is it?"

Katrina nods. "I'm looking at you now, aren't I? In a moment I won't be. I'm just your roommate. It's not like I know where you are all the time, right?"

"Great. Thanks. I'm going to slip out through the pool emergency exit." As I pick up my luggage, I think about Jake. Part of me wants to say good-bye and part of me wants to kick him in the shins for possibly collaborating on Matthew Hartnett's plan. If I found him, things could get ugly. Or they could end up like they had in the pool or behind the blow-up during V-ball. That's how things were with Jake—I could never fully know what was going to happen. So I decide to let it go.

"Good luck," Katrina says to me.

"And Katrina . . ."

"Yes?"

"Be good to yourself. You're bigger and better than ballet—in a good way—and don't you ever forget it!" are my final words, as I leave room 20 for the very last time.

★ ★ ★

I manage to make it out the pool's emergency exit without anyone seeing me and then half run, half walk down to the lake. I skim the edge rather than use the lit-up driveway, in case I'm seen. I slip through the trees that line the path and, finally, get to the large gates. Still hidden, I search in my backpack until I've found my cell, then switch it on, hoping it'll work now that I'm so close to the main road.

I don't know what kind of interference system they're using at the retreat, but it's good. I'd tried my cell several times during my short stay, and it had never worked. But now it powers up and dings all the right dings at me. And within the next minute or two I've secured myself a cab to the airport.

While I wait for my ride, I call the airline Melissa has booked my return ticket on and cross my fingers that (a) there's a decent flight out tonight and that (b) it isn't full. As it turns out, I'm in luck. There's a seat available for me on a flight that's leaving in less than two hours. After it's set, I put in a quick call to Melissa and cross my fingers. Obviously the crossing-the-fingers thing works, because I get her voice mail, just like I'd wanted.

I leave a message. "I know what's going on, Melissa. Check me out of the retreat. I'm on my way home. We'll talk when I get back."

And then I turn off my phone. Because, right now, I don't want to talk to Melissa or anyone else.

Right now, what I need is time to think.

★ ★ ★

My brain does that crazy all-over-the-place thing again as the cabbie drives me to the airport. One second I'm thinking maybe Mannie's right and that I should call my dad, then I'm off on a tangent of how I'm going to play things out with Melissa, and only milliseconds after that, I'm wondering if there'll be anything decent to eat at the airport at this time of night.

I can't concentrate on anything for longer than fifteen seconds, let alone form any kind of decent plan.

Which makes me wonder if I should call my dad again and . . .

Aaaggghhh!

So I try to concentrate on other things for the rest of the trip. I count people, dogs, and red lights. I force myself to sing along in my head to the terrible golden oldies radio station the driver is listening to. I flick a hangnail back and forth until it hurts. Anything to distract me from the other thing—which I'm starting to realize is less Melissa based and more Jake based. What's he going to think when he realizes I've disappeared?

Finally, we get to Logan Airport. With my bag checked, security negotiated, and my boarding pass held very, very tightly in my hand, I get to my gate and just want to lie down on the floor in relief.

I've made it.

I'm going home.

I take a look at the floor, wonder how I ever thought about lying on it, and pick out a slightly less dirty chair to collapse into, dropping my backpack beneath my legs.

Ahhh.

Again, I force myself not to think too hard. I don't want to wind up talking to myself or looking in any way insane when I've gotten this far—I'd probably end up having some well-meaning flight attendant not allow me on board. I concentrate on slowly breathing in and out and staring at the ceiling. I just need a few Zenlike moments to collect myself. Which is no surprise, really. After all, it's been a vicious couple days.

Hmmm. Maybe that's not entirely true. My normal work is a lot more vicious. This was more . . . an emotional roller coaster. Usually I'm in and out, running around, darting from one location and tip-off to the next. Not to mention squeezing in that thing they call school during the daylight hours. But this—immersing myself in a ruse—it was harder than I'd thought. Maybe I should cut those actors a break sometime.

Still, I guess I will be in a way, if I'm getting out of this game once and for all. First things first, though. Get home and see how I can squeeze as much money out of Melissa as possible. I don't feel like thinking about the money, but I know I need to. For school. As for Jake and his feelings, I need to push them to one side for the moment. I can't think past confronting Melissa right now. Everything's going to ride on that, and focusing on what could happen beyond it is simply too complex.

I push myself up a bit in the seat just as a guy sitting across from me cracks open a bottle of cola, which reminds me of the cola contract, and I stare at the soda and think of Ned. The real Ned. Which is more than slightly confusing, because Jake is really *my* Ned. The Ned who'd been good to me, who'd picked me up when I was hurt, who'd lectured me, who'd given me the whole idea of disguising myself, which led to me being at the retreat to spy on him being Ned. The Ned who made me forget about work all the time and forced me to think about other things. Him, mainly.

I shake my head, dislodging this thought, and then realize, while I'm staring at the soda bottle, that I could really, really go for something similar myself. Not a cola contract (like that's going to happen!) but a drink of some kind. So, with a sigh, I get up, grab my backpack, and head for the food court. On the way, my eyes zip through the crowd on autopilot, just checking to see if there's anyone worth grabbing a shot of.

It takes me some time to recognize what I'm doing and I stop myself. I don't need to do this anymore. I'm out, remember? Out, out, out. But I can't seem to help it. It's a behavior that is ingrained in me now. So I look at people's midsections, legs, and shoes and at the floor as I go, trying not to care who they are. I don't even look up to the face of whoever's wearing that very flashy pair of Louboutin boots.

And I've just bought my bottle of water and am uncapping it, turning to head back toward my gate, when I hear the voice coming from the other side of the baked potato stand to my left and every single hair on my arms stands straight on end.

"Can you put extra bacon bits on that?"

"I thought you were cutting back?" I round the cart in seconds. Even with a baseball cap pulled on low for anonymity, I recognize him easily (a paparazzo skill).

"Jo?!" Jake does a double take. "What the . . . ?"

"That'll be six ninety," the baked potato guy says, and Jake turns to look at him as if he's an alien speaking a different language.

"Six ninety? Oh, oh right. Sure. Here." He hunts in his pocket and passes the guy some money.

"Nice seeing you again . . . Jake." I finally get to use his real name. The baked potato guy raises his head on hearing the cold tone in my voice, and I shoot him a look and grab Jake's arm. I drag him a few steps over until we're next to a free table. "Sit," I tell him, making sure I guide him to the seat that faces the wall. We don't need any extra attention.

He sits obediently.

"Nice of you to say good-bye." I sit down as well, then take a long swig of my water.

When I look at Jake again, he's almost laughing. "I guess I could say the same to you!"

Hmmm, okay. Fair enough. "What are you doing here?"

"I'm going back to LA."

"Next flight?" I raise an eyebrow.

After a second or two, Jake inclines his head slightly. "You, too?" he finally asks me.

I nod slowly as well. It doesn't look like either of us wants to give too much away too quickly.

A few moments pass in silence. Finally, Jake opens his mouth, closes it, and then hesitates just a little more before he speaks. "But you only got to the retreat a couple days ago. Did you check yourself out? Just now?"

I shrug. "Sort of. Did you?"

Jake looks kind of cagey. "I, um, spoke to my dad."

I don't say anything, opting to just watch him closely. Will he admit to being in on Matthew Hartnett's plan? Jake looks uncomfortable, but he continues. "Some things came out."

"Like?"

Jake stabs his overloaded baked potato with his fork but doesn't eat any. "I told him someone had realized I wasn't Ned."

"Which would be me."

Jake nods but doesn't look up. "And then he told me some stuff. Stuff that I didn't know was going on and didn't want to hear. So I left."

My heart starts beating a whole lot faster in my chest. Wow. Jake really *doesn't* know about his dad's grand plan. Or at least he didn't until earlier this evening. "What did he tell you?" I ask.

Jake still doesn't look up. "He was just . . . using me. Again."

"What did he tell you, Jake?" The words spill out of my mouth too fast.

He looks up at me now, straight into my eyes. "He told me he'd set up even more than me just being there at the retreat. He told me he'd hired some photographer. Some paparazzo! And that they'd been there, at the retreat. As in, shooting me being Ned the whole time. He had a deal with some paper lined up. You know, just once, I thought he could do the right thing by Ned. Just once. But no . . . he's sick. He's a sick man."

There's a long silence in which Jake stares everywhere but at me. "So, who do you think it is?" he finally says when his eyes move back to meet mine. "It's got to be one of the counselors, doesn't it? Do you think it's Brad?" He bites his lip for a second, wondering. "It's just that he made such a big deal about 'outsiders' at that circus-skills thing, remember? Or what about Seth? Even if that was a real pen he had the other night, the whole thing was kind of weird . . . ," he says, trailing off.

I stare back at him without moving a muscle. "I don't think it's Brad, Jake. And I don't think it's Seth, either."

"But who, then?" He frowns.

I keep staring at him, motionless. Expressionless. Until I realize he's not going to put two and two together. He's practically looking straight through me. "You don't remember, do you?" I blurt out.

"Remember what?"

I pause for a second, wondering if it's wise to continue, but then I keep going, not caring. I'm sick of all the lies and the game playing. I'm tired of having to think so hard every time I go to open my mouth. I may as well tell the truth for once. And I *want* to tell Jake the truth. He's a good guy who doesn't deserve any of this. "You don't remember picking me up off the ground. Lecturing me."

"At the circus skills workshop?" Jake keeps right on frowning.

I sigh. "No, not at the circus skills workshop. In LA. I cracked my elbow. Outside some restaurant. You picked me up. You, not Ned, though I thought you were Ned at the time. You asked me where my parents were and I gave you some lip and . . . well, you were there. You know the rest. I know now it wasn't Ned. It was you."

Another beat or two of noncomprehension passes before I can see the realization practically flood through every cell in Jake's body. "Wait. Wait. Are you saying that was *you*? That you were the kid I picked up off the pavement?"

I take another swig of water. I nod.

"But no . . . it wasn't . . . you . . . I . . ."

And it's almost too painful waiting for the end result, so I push him toward the truth with a big fat shove in the hope of getting it over and done with quickly. Kind of like tying a loose tooth to a piece of string and a doorknob. "What I'm saying, Jake, is that it's me. I'm the paparazzo your father has been paying to spy on you."

chapter 18

"What?!" Jake stands up, almost pushing over the whole table in the process. "You? That's who he's talking about? That's who he hired? *You?!?!*"

"Sit down!" I hiss at him, my eyes shooting daggers. "Unless you want some other paparazzo spotting you."

Jake sits, his mouth set in a hard line and his eyes not wavering from mine.

I stare back at him wearily. "I take it you remember me now. So, I was right. It was you that night."

He gives me a dirty look and a huff in return. "Yeah, I was there. I just couldn't see the resemblance. I mean, I thought that was a kid. A funny-looking kid with braces and baggy clothes and . . . I could barely tell you were a girl."

"Gee, thanks. I'm glad you changed your opinion on that one. Unless you regularly kiss people you can barely tell are girls."

I get another look for this and shake my head at Jake in reply. "Don't look at me like that. For a start, you were lying as much as I was, and, anyway, this is exactly the kind of thing you told me to do, isn't it? You told me I had a 'distinct advantage' and that I should use it. Well, here I am. Thanks to your timely advice."

"I . . ." Jake frowns, then shrugs.

"You can't deny you told me to take this path." I point a finger and sit forward in my seat. "Don't get me wrong, you've got every right to hate me. Hey, I hate me right now. The editor who's in cahoots with your dad hates me right now. And I'm pretty sure Brad won't be lining up to be my best friend, either, when he realizes who I really am. Feel free to join the crowd. But don't you sit there and think this has been some easy ride for me. I didn't want to take this job. I took it because I had to. I need the money for school. But now . . . well, I don't know what's going to happen moneywise. I wish I'd never said yes and had kept on doing the paparazzo thing for another six months or even a year, if that's what it took. I could have handled that. This was obviously just too much."

Jake stares at me for a while. "What do you mean? That this could have been your last job?"

"Maybe. The money was good. It would have meant

I could at least cut back enough to stop falling asleep in class."

"Staying awake in class always helps. Do you do that a lot?"

I sigh. "Let's just say there's a lot of drool stains on my textbooks."

"So why didn't you want to take the job?"

I get straight to the point, looking directly into Jake's eyes. "Because of you, of course."

"Me?"

I feel my cheeks go hot and distract myself by taking another swig of water from my bottle. "Yes, you."

"What about me?"

I look away.

"Well?" Jake isn't going to let it go.

I turn back. "Out of everyone in Hollywood it had to be you. Not even Ned you, but *you* you."

"You you? You're not making a whole lot of sense."

"I am in my head," I mutter. What does he need me to do here? Stand up on the table and yell, "Hello! Hot guy! I'm into you!"

Or maybe not, because Jake has a definite smirk on his face that looks like he's enjoying watching me squirm. Just like that smirk he'd given me when we were playing V-ball. The one he gave me right before we kissed . . .

"So what you're saying is that it made a difference that it wasn't Ned you had to take shots of at the retreat, but me?"

I'm trapped. "Look, all I'm saying is that you were . . . good to me that night. And I haven't forgotten it. So, um . . . thanks." I mumble this last part.

"But you still took photos of me, or Ned me at the retreat?"

I'm not sure what to say. I take a deep breath. "I took . . . a few. Before I realized what was going on. And before I realized I was part of something much larger. But I haven't done anything with them."

"Hold on." Jake sits up straight. "You haven't sold them? And you haven't sent them to anyone?"

"No."

Jake shakes his head. "Look, I'm not quite sure what's going on. How this is all working. Is my dad paying you directly to be here, or what?"

Over the next few minutes, as Jake wolfs down his baked potato (and, yes, extra bacon bits), I fill him in on the whole Melissa–Matthew Hartnett deal. Jake whistles when he hears how much I'm being paid.

"Wow! That is some amount. You must be pretty good, huh?"

I do a quick sweep of my body with one hand. "Like you mentioned, I have an advantage. And I charge for it. They could hardly have sent some forty-year-old hairy-faced pap in, could they?"

"I guess not."

Silence.

"So, um, you're not angry at me?" I eventually ask.

Across the table, Jake thinks about my question for a while. Then he shrugs. "To be fair, what you said was true—I've told you as many lies as you've told me; you just had a little more insider info about what was really going on. Plus, you're cute."

I try to act cool about this. "I guess you're right. On both counts."

Jake laughs. "You know, if we want to be smart about this, we should probably turn our energy to being angry at the people who've been lying to us from the beginning."

I consider his words. "That makes a lot of sense." I watch as Jake looks down at his plate, then dives in to take the last bite of his baked potato. "I really should have paid more attention when the guy was making that. It's probably going to be my next job."

"Taking shots of baked potatoes? Do you want to get into food photography or something?"

I laugh. "No, that's not what I meant. I meant because I'm going to be making them. Or flipping burgers. Or something similar. 'Sure you don't want fries with that, sir?'"

Jake laughs. "You don't want to be the queen of super-sizing? So what do you really want to do then?"

"Well, probably what I was hinting at the other night. The change I want to make—it's school. I'm saving so I can study portrait photography. That's why I took this job."

"Until my dad messed it up for you," Jake humphs. "Sorry he had to weasel his way into your life, too."

I shrug.

"Wait a second, I just got an idea." Jake holds up a hand, and there's silence as he pauses and thinks for a minute or two. Finally, he looks me straight in the eye. "You've still got the shots of me, right? You didn't delete them. And you're not a fan of this Melissa chick, right?"

I shake my head. Then nod, not sure of the right answer to the question. "What I'm saying is, yes, I have the shots. And no, I'm definitely not a fan of this Melissa chick."

"And I'm not a fan of what my dad's been up to."

I snort. "Me, neither."

Jake pauses again, then grins. "We're two reasonably smart people, yes?"

"I know I am. I'm not sure about you and your bacon bit obsession, though."

"Very funny. Maybe I can prove it to you. How about if we found a solution to both our problems? I make sure Ned gets the treatment he really needs, not this quick patch-up and cover-up that I never wanted to be part of in the first place, and you get the money you need to pay for your classes, without having to turn into baked potato girl."

"Sounds good to me."

"Okay then, let's get planning. First step, those shots. Show me what you've got . . ."

Naturally, Jake isn't all that impressed with my shots. Especially the one where his finger has taken on a life of its own.

"I was so not picking my nose!" he says loudly, making at least three or four tables surrounding us turn and stare.

"Sorry," he mumbles. "But I wasn't." He decides he's going to leave stardom to his more photogenic, less itchy-nosed brother from now on.

Finally it's time to board the plane. Jake and I get settled, then almost immediately get upgraded to business class when he pulls off his baseball cap and a flight attendant thinks he's Ned.

Kind of ironic, but neither of us exactly rushes to correct her.

It takes us less than half an hour to come up with a simple plan that covers the three key goals we're most concerned about:

1. WE PROTECT NED THROUGH ALL OF THIS. HE NEEDS HIS TREATMENT AND BOTH OF US ARE GOING TO MAKE SURE HE GETS IT;

2. I GET OUT OF THIS WITHOUT PAPPING ANOTHER DAY. THERE WILL NEED TO BE MONEY INVOLVED SOMEHOW, AND IT WILL HAVE TO BE ENOUGH TO MEET THE COST OF SCHOOL; AND

3. JAKE FINDS HIS OWN TREATMENT FOR THE BACON-BITS THING (HE ADDS IN THIS EXTRA POINT AFTER HAVING TO LOOSEN HIS BELT A NOTCH, POST—BAKED POTATO).

With our plan formulated, I then spend the rest of the flight quizzing Jake about Ned. Neither of us wants to lie anymore, but we both know that for money to be involved, there will need to be shots of Ned. The real Ned, that is. And that's part of the plan—Jake asks me to take them. But if I want to take good ones—great ones—I need to know everything about Ned.

Everything.

So Jake sets out to tell me. And we talk and talk and talk all the long way back to LA.

We're sitting in our seats devouring breakfast when Jake pauses for a moment and turns to me. "You know, I think we could actually pull this off," he says, shock in his voice.

"Me, too." I glance out of the window. "Hey, look." I touch Jake on the arm.

"Dawn," he says, spotting the very first rays of sun in the sky. "A new day," he says slowly.

I glance at him for a second. "Yep, a new day." I nod, knowing exactly what he means. And it's in this moment, looking at Jake, realizing that this is it—this is my new life, my new way of living, my new everything—that I know what I have to do.

I have to return Matthew Hartnett's money.

All of it. Every last cent.

I hadn't told Jake that his father had already paid me part of the money for this job. I don't know why—force of habit, I suppose. I'm not used to full disclosure (when I think

219

this, Seth's face pops into my head and says, "Trust issues, much?"). But the thing is, those shots—I know that by keeping Matthew Hartnett's money, they're really his. And even if we take better shots of Ned and manage to pull off our plan, you never know with Matthew Hartnett. If he gets hold of those other shots (most likely by siccing his lawyers on me), he'll hand them straight over to Melissa, who'll run the worst ones. Maybe even before we get a chance to put our plan into action.

Melissa wouldn't hesitate to run the shots of Jake making a fool of himself at circus school, falling off the low wire, spinning plates with a confused expression on his face, juggling badly with balls bouncing off his head. Or the one of him shoveling bacon bits in his mouth as if he's on a food bender. Or the not very flattering one of him concentrating, his tongue sticking out of his mouth slightly, in pottery class. It wouldn't matter to her that by doing this she'd be jeopardizing the real Ned's future.

I am so over being controlled like a puppet by the Melissas and Matthews of the world. Just this once, I am going to control how this plays out. I am going to say who runs my shots, when they run them, and how they run them. No one is going to get played or screwed over or lied to. Not Ned. Not me. And not Jake, either. So, Matthew Hartnett wants these shots plastered all over the papers? Well, just for once, he isn't going to get what he wants. He's going to get what his son *needs*, instead. Ned is going to get what he needs—treatment for his phobia without having to lie about it. I am going to get what I need—getting out of this game and starting to work on what I really love. And Jake is going to get what he needs—exiting all this ridiculousness with his pride intact.

The only problem is . . .

. . . pulling it all off.

I turn my head away from Jake and pretend I'm looking out the window, but I'm not. I'm staring at my reflection instead, my anger dissipating by the second. I just don't see how I can afford to give Matthew Hartnett's money back. I mean, we'll be able to make some money on the new shots, but probably not as much as I'll need for school.

Then again, I don't see how I can afford *not* to give the money back. My new start won't be much of a new start if I know it's based on lies and cheating and falsehood and doing the wrong thing by people I care about.

So close, yet so far.

As I stare out the window, tears well up in my eyes. I just want to get out now. Why does it have to be so crazily hard? I remember Mannie's advice about keeping my emotions out of all this, but I can't do it. This isn't business anymore. It's about people I know. People I like. And respect. Or one person, anyway. And I must sniff or something at this point of wallowing in my own misery, because Jake reaches out for my hand.

"Jo? You okay?"

I glance at him for just a second before I lean back on my headrest and close my eyes. "I'm just tired, Jake." And that's the truth—I'm so very, very tired. Not just physically but emotionally as well. I'm so very, very tired of lying and hiding and cheating and pretending. I'm tired of my whole life.

I keep holding on to his hand. I grasp it tight, hoping he'll never ask me to let go.

★ ★ ★

Jake and I manage to get an hour or so of sleep before the plane lands. In the cab back to my place, we go over our delegated duties again. And it's not a lot, but it will take some planning, a few phone calls, and a whole lot of luck.

By the time we get to my apartment, we think we have it all covered. We've developed a plan.

A foolproof one, we hope.

Still, even if it isn't foolproof (I expect nothing can be when Matthew Hartnett is involved), I'm pretty sure we can do this.

There's only one little thing that could mess it up. Something I haven't told Jake about, though I'm preparing to spring it on him as soon as we get to my apartment.

"Just over there," I say to the driver as we make our way up my street. "Number two twenty-seven."

He swings over to the curb.

"I guess this is you," Jake says.

"Um, can you come up for a second?" I say, then blush.

"Um, that sounded bad. I mean, just for a second. I have to . . . show you something. I mean, do something. That I want you to see." Oh man. Could that have sounded worse?

"Sure," Jake says. "Should I get the cab to wait?"

I nod. "It'll only take a minute or two. Really."

Just as we're making our way upstairs in the dawn light, I see Wendy locking her front door. I'd texted her as soon as our plane landed to tell her I was back at LAX, and she'd texted back to say she'd be on her way out there herself. It looks like we've just caught her.

"Hi, lovely cuz!" she calls out from upstairs as she parks her small bag beside her, snapping the handle down smartly. "Good timing!" She walks over to the top of the stairs to meet me in the half dark, her heels clicking as she goes.

"Oh, hello." She nods when we get up to the landing and she finally sees Jake standing next to me. Even though Jake is tall, Wendy seems to tower above him in her high heels and her streamlined camel-colored uniform, her French twist and pillbox hat on top of her head elongating her neck and making her look even taller.

"Wendy, this is Jake. Jake, my cousin Wendy."

Wendy gives me an odd look and a raised eyebrow. Because I know her so well, I know exactly what she's saying to me without her uttering a word. "Um, hun," her eyebrow tells me, "this isn't Jake. This is Ned Hartnett. Have you bumped your head on the pavement again tonight? Need me to take you to the emergency room? And, by the way, would you care to explain why you have a male of the species entering your apartment at this hour of the morning? Hmmm?"

"It's okay," I half laugh at her. "His name really is Jake. And the other thing's okay, too."

Now Wendy frowns as if to say, "Did they give you a lobotomy at that retreat?"

I sigh. "To be more exact, Jake Hartnett. Ned Hartnett's brother."

Jake laughs and lifts up the bottom of his shirt slightly. "See? No scar!"

"Riiiiight," Wendy nods and says, "I see."

"It's a long story, Wendy," I say, turning my key in the lock and pushing the front door open. "A long, long, long, long story." I turn around to see her cross her arms.

"In which you're still sixteen and it's"—she checks her watch—"not yet six in the morning."

I shoot her a look. "It's all fine, Wendy, like I said."

Jake nods at her. "I'm a good guy. No funny business."

Wendy pauses, then laughs. "Sure, because I haven't heard that one before!"

"Come in with us then," I say to Wendy as I enter the apartment.

She pauses and checks her watch. "Well, okay. I have a few minutes."

I don't look back. Instead I dump my bag and go over to

power up my desktop. Within thirty seconds, I'm sitting at my computer.

Okay, this is it.

Hold on to your horses, Jake.

With a deep breath, I go to my banking site and type in my username and password. As my account loads up, I have to take another breath. If I'm not careful, I'll probably hyperventilate, but I need all the help I can get right now. My head isn't 100 percent sure what I'm doing is the right thing.

But my heart is.

"Okay, here goes nothing. This is what I wanted you to see, Jake. Come on, Wendy. You can be a witness."

"To . . . ?" Wendy asks as she and Jake both step forward.

"Giving back Jake's dad's money," I say. "Because he's already paid me some. Ready?" I click on a few buttons and then I'm set. "The money goes in and the money goes . . . out." I refresh my banking details. "There. It's gone."

Wow. It really is gone. I note the numbers that flash up on the screen. That money is so, so gone. Oh, please, let me have done the right thing. Let there be a way out of this. For everyone involved.

I start to take yet another deep breath but then stop myself short. Because I realize something. It's not just the money that's disappeared.

So has my guilt. All of a sudden, I feel this sort of . . . lightness. Like part of my worry has disappeared along with the money. And there's something else, too. A sense that everything will be okay. That I really will find a way out of this. And so will Jake. And Ned.

When I glance up, Wendy looks confused, but she must see what my actions mean to both me and Jake because of the expressions on our faces. She looks from me to him, assesses what's going on, then stands up and leans back. "Well, I have no idea what that was about, or why you're giving away perfectly good money, but it was powerful, Jo. Powerful."

"Thanks, Wendy."

Beside her, Jake simply nods and remains silent. I can't tell if he's angry, happy, or just in shock . . . or anything, really.

"One last thing before you go," I say. "And this one you actually know about." I nod at Jake. "Time to put the plan into action." I grab my cell and bring up the right number for an after-hours call to one of my best contacts—another newspaper editor. One I actually kind of like. Maybe even trust a little bit. "Mitchell?" I say when he picks up. "Sorry to call you at this time of the morning, but I've got something for you. Something big . . ."

After my call to Mitchell, Jake picks up his bag. "I'd better go," he says. "I've kept that cab waiting forever. Nice meeting you, Wendy."

"You, too, Jake. Stay one of the good guys, will you?"

226

Jake laughs. "I'll try!"

"I'll be back in a second to fill you in," I tell Wendy as I follow Jake out onto the landing.

He pauses at the top of the steps, looking slightly uncomfortable, moving from foot to foot. "Look, Jo . . . about the money. It's just that . . . I mean, thanks. Thanks, but you didn't have to do that. It's too much to ask, with school and everything—"

"But you didn't ask," I cut in. "I had to do it, Jake. For me."

"But what if the money we get from our plan isn't enough?"

I shrug. "It'll just have to be. Or I'll change my plans slightly. Or really look into that flipping-burgers thing. All I know is, I couldn't get that new start on your dad's money. It wasn't right."

Jake and I stare at each other. "It's a big deal, Jo," he finally says. "A huge deal. It means a lot to me that you're doing this. For me and for Ned, you know?"

I nod. "I know."

"I guess maybe it's worth trusting people you barely know sometimes?"

I laugh, thinking back to my circus skills tantrum. "Maybe," I say, then feel a bit braver in the half light. "It helps if they're gorgeous." Eek! Where did that come from?

I hold my breath, waiting for Jake's reply. Which, thankfully, doesn't seem to include screaming, "Freak!" and running away down the stairs. Instead, he smiles, but it's kind of a tired smile. Thankfully, the cab driver honks, which is a welcome distraction.

"I'd better go." Jake waves to the cabbie, telling him he's coming. "Thanks again, Jo. I really mean that." He bends forward and kisses me. And even though it's quick, my legs almost start shaking. Before he can move away, though, I kiss him back. I'm not missing opportunities to do *that* again.

When Jake finally pulls back, he smiles again. He still looks worn out, but I'm glad to see it doesn't look like he's tired of me. "Okay, so give me twenty-four hours to pull these meetings together, and I'll pick you up tomorrow. Two o'clock, right?" he says as he gives one of my shoulders a final squeeze and then starts for the stairs.

"Yep. Two," I reply. Two. Which should just give me time to get a few hours' rest, catch up on the work e-mails I've neglected while I've been at the retreat, deal with the Wicked Witch of West Hollywood (part of my delegated duties), meet Mannie for lunch tomorrow—as promised during our last IM session—and be home again that afternoon to pull off the rest of Jake's and my (fingers crossed) foolproof plan.

chapter 19

I text Melissa around 9:00 a.m. the same day. When I get to the diner at 11:00, as arranged, she's waiting for me. As I walk toward her I can see by the expression on her face that, today, there will be no happy cherry pie orders or girly chitchat.

Today will be all business.

I take my time in getting over to her and sitting down on the opposite side of the booth.

"Well? Where are my shots?" is all she says. She gives me a slow once-over, noting the absence of my backpack. "Wait. You don't have any, do you?"

"Oh, I have shots." I pause dramatically and spend some

time getting comfortable in my seat, enjoying every milli-second of this. "I have plenty of shots. I have juggling shots and balancing shots, shots of formal group time and infor-mal group time chatting on the lawn. I have shots of him talking to girls at lunch and pensive ones of him on his own."

"Well, where are they?"

"Where are what?"

Melissa looks as if steam is about to come out of her ears. "The shots of Ned, of course."

I try to act confused. "Wait, I never said I had shots of Ned. I do, however, have plenty of shots of Ned's brother, Jake."

"Oh. I see." Melissa eyes me for a moment, her mouth set in a hard line. "You found out. So what? Look, I'm sorry if you feel a bit used, but I knew the shots would be better if you didn't know. More realistic. So, hand them over. I take it you have a Memory Stick with you. Or did you e-mail?"

"Um . . . no. I don't have a Memory Stick. And I didn't e-mail. And I'm not going to, either."

Across the table from me, Melissa frowns as hard as her Botoxed forehead will allow. "What's that supposed to mean?"

"I don't think you're getting this, Melissa. I'm not going to give you those shots. Ever. I only came here today to let you know that all the money's been transferred back. Not to you, but to ML Entertainment." I stand up, done almost as soon as I'd started. "I also wanted to let you know I won't be working with you again."

Melissa laughs a croaky laugh. "And you expect me to care? Want to play games with me, little girl? When this gets around, you won't be working with *anyone* again."

Perfect. "Which suits me just fine." I grin as, before me, Melissa tries to frown even harder, not understanding what's going on and why I don't care if I never pap again.

"And you dragged me down here to tell me this because . . . ?"

Now it's me who laughs. "Because otherwise, Melissa, I wouldn't have been able to see the look on your face." I wave my fingers as I depart. "Toodles, dahling!"

★ ★ ★

"Jo?" I get the call from Mannie just as I'm peddling away on my bike.

"Hang on," I say, pulling over beside a telephone pole, which will hopefully stop Melissa if she suddenly decides to veer into me with her convertible. "Sorry," I say, when I finally jump off. "Just dodging Melissa. All good now. We still on for lunch?"

"That's why I'm calling," Mannie says in a kind of half whisper.

"You busy?"

"Sort of. But we can still meet if you're up for a bit of waiting around."

"Hey, I'm pretty used to it. I can probably handle some more of the same."

"Great. You know that solarium that we've cased before? The one just off Sunset?"

"Sure." I nod, even though Mannie can't see me. We'd sat there for hours one day, broiling in the sun, waiting for someone who turned out only to be a look-alike. Meanwhile, a number of other high-profile stars were getting booted out of the Mondrian, and we both missed the whole thing.

"Can you meet me there?"

"Sure can. See you in twenty."

"You said 'toodles, dahling?' to Melissa?" Mannie glances away from the entrance to the solarium for only a second before he turns his attention back again, worried he'll miss his target. I can tell he's impressed, though. If he hadn't been, his eyes would have stayed put on the door.

"I did," I say. "And it was quite satisfying, too." I put my backpack down on the ground for a second and rummage around in it, pulling out the two bottles of water I'd stopped to buy along the way. "Here you go." I uncap one and pass it over to Mannie.

"Thanks, Jo. I won't ask how you knew I'd need this . . ."

"Oh, I knew all right." I don't have to tell Mannie about all the afternoons I've spent baking in the sun. He's been there and done that. In fact, he's doing it right now as we perch half on the curb and half behind a rental car, ready to pounce.

I watch as he puts his water down and brings up his

camera. "Come to me, my little fried dumpling. I can see the headlines already."

"Fried dumpling?"

"Maybe I'm hungry," Mannie says. "I hope you're not. Hungry for shots, I mean. I thought you said you were getting out?"

"Hey, I've come without ammo. It's a weird feeling, but I'm cameraless. So, who is it?"

Mannie names an up-and-coming young star. "I wouldn't be surprised if it is her. She has been known to tan. Remember those shots from the UK?"

I nod. "Yep. They were everywhere."

"Naughty girl, tanning. And Mommy took her, too. Don't get it, myself. Why risk skin cancer when there's a spray-tanning place on every corner?"

I shrug. "And let's not forget—melanomas are so last year."

Mannie snorts a loud snort. "That would make a great headline. But stop making me lose concentration."

"Sorry. I can go if that helps."

"Don't be crazy. Anyway, we're not done with the Melissa thing yet." Without breaking his gaze on the solarium entry-way, he reaches out and punches me in the arm with spectacular accuracy. "It's not every day someone tells Melissa they don't have the shots she wants and then tells her 'toodles.' But you did. And I'm proud of you, man."

I laugh and give my arm a rub. "Thanks, Mannie."

We both hold our breath as someone exits the solarium. Nope. Not her.

Mannie lowers his camera. "I would've paid a million bucks to see you say that to Melissa. Not that I have a million bucks. Do you think anyone would ever offer a million bucks for these shots?" A dreamy expression comes over his face.

"No, Mannie. I hate to burst your bubble, but I don't."

"Me, either. But I can dream, right?" He shrugs, still focused on the solarium.

"We can all dream, Mannie."

He nods. "And you got your dream. You're getting out, Jo. For good. I'm gonna miss you, man." Mannie reaches over now for another punch on the arm, but I manage to jump out of the way in time, and he punches thin air.

Even with that one missed punch, I think I'm going to have a bruise after our clandestine solarium meeting today. Still, it's one I'll wear with pride. I think it's against the paparazzo code of conduct to have things like friends about your person, but Mannie's never cared. "Thanks again for helping me out with the advice the other night," I say. "I was really losing the plot there for a while."

"S'okay," Mannie says. He raises his camera again as a shadow falls on the doorway, but it's just someone moving around inside.

"No, it was really good of you. I'll never forget it."

Mannie's eyebrows raise at this. "Doesn't take much to

impress you, does it?" He reaches down blindly for his water, finds it, and lifts it up to his mouth to take a swig.

"Not after a couple years in this game, no. I don't think I realized how entrenched I was. I'm going to be very, very glad to get out. Not that there's anything wrong with it. It's just not for me."

He nods. "Yeah, I hear you. Hey, I was wondering—speaking of getting out . . ." He looks over at me for a second.

This must be serious. "Yeeeeesssss . . . ," I say, knowing something is going on in that mussed-haired head of his.

His eyes meet mine again. "I was sort of wondering if you're going to sell any of your stuff."

I give Mannie a slow once-over, my mouth twisted to one side. I look down all six feet two inches of him. "Think you can pass for eleven like me?"

He laughs again. "Maybe. If I take a skateboard and bend my knees. So . . . ?"

I shake my head. "No."

"Ah well, just thought I'd check." Mannie shrugs.

I pause for a moment or two until the silence forces him to look at me. And then I quit leaning on the rental car and reach across to give him a good punch in the arm. "I'm not selling my stuff, Mannie, I'm giving it."

Now it's Mannie who pauses. "What do you mean? To me?" He's completely, utterly, and totally ignoring the solarium now.

"Of course you, you idiot!"

"Like your fauxPod and everything?"

"Everything, Mannie. It's all yours."

"Wow!" He continues to stare at me.

"Mannie!" I gesture as someone exits the solarium.

Mannie's attention zips back to the doorway, and he's shooting before we even get a decent look at who it is. As it turns out, it's not her. "Phew." He breathes a sigh of relief and his eyes return to mine once more. "But you could sell it. Your stuff, I mean."

"I don't want to sell it. I want to give it to you."

Beside me, Mannie shakes his head as if I'm crazy. "You sure?"

I laugh. "Yes, I'm sure."

"Really sure?"

"Really sure. Though, if you ask me one more time, I might sell it, after all. To someone who annoys me less."

Mannie zips his lips and throws away the key behind one shoulder, which makes me laugh at him. "Sometimes you're so high school," I say.

"Well, so are you!" he retorts.

"Yes, but that's okay, seeing as I'm *in* high school. Remember?"

Mannie chuckles. "Huh. That's true. Sometimes I forget that. Anyway, thanks for the gear, man. Appreciate it."

And I appreciate you, Mannie, I think, but instead of saying the words, I wink. And he winks back. Some things don't need to be spoken out loud.

Mannie's attention returns to the solarium, and it's a while before he says anything again. "So what's your dad think about all this? About you getting out?"

"Is this your roundabout way of asking if I've called him yet?"

Mannie flicks me a sideways glance and grins. "Yeah, maybe. Am I that transparent?"

"Yes. Look, to be honest, I haven't told him." I know I should. I know I have to. I just haven't done it yet. "I don't think you get it. Last time I spoke to him, from the retreat, he basically told me I'd never get out. That I was born to do this. He just doesn't know me at all."

"Nah, he's wrong if he thinks that. You were born to shoot, but you never really loved this game. Not like your dad."

"Well, he has problems accepting that."

Mannie laughs. "Of course he does! You're his little girl. He just wants to think you're like him, that's all. It's his way of being your dad. Can't you see that?"

"If he wanted to be my father so badly, don't you think he'd be better off supporting what I really want to do?"

"But he is," Mannie says. "He's paying half, isn't he?"

I squirm against the rental car, and not because it's getting hotter by the second. "Well . . . yes."

"That's pretty supportive, isn't it?"

"I guess," I mumble, glad he isn't looking at me right now. This is feeling all too much like I'm back in group.

"I know he's not always here and stuff, not like some

people's parents who are around way too much," Mannie says, rolling his eyes. "But you've got to give him some credit, Jo. He's a good guy. I, um, haven't really told you, but before he left for Japan, he gave me his number. I've called him a few times when I've needed info on someone or a tip. He always gets back to me. Right away. He's a good guy, your dad. Maybe he doesn't know how to show it to you all the time. He's just not a talker. But you know something? It was even your dad who gave me this lead. He's got some-one on the inside here who gives him tip-offs."

I take in Mannie's words silently. I know a lot of what he's saying is true. Dad has always had a lot of time for Mannie. But compliments about my dad can be hard to hear when I'm dealing with my own stuff about him. At the same time, if there's one thing I see now from my time at the retreat, it's to try and look deeper. There's always a reason for people's actions. "It is what it is" is nothing more than a patchy cover-up.

"When you pull this off—and I'm saying 'when' not 'if' because I know you—you should give your dad a call. Really fill him in. Maybe he's just worried that if you stop papping, he'll lose that connection with you, you know?"

"Yeah, maybe." I sigh. In the silence that follows, I change my position against the rental car once more. And I'm just about to tell Mannie that I'll need to head out soon when I see the rolling glimmer of something black and shiny out of the corner of one eye. Like a meerkat, I'm instantly on my feet, head swiveling. I can't see the car anymore, but I know my instincts are still good. That was a town car I saw. I just know it.

"There's something going on," I say to Mannie. "There's no back entrance, is there?" I remember that from the last time we were here. Of course we always check the back entrances before setting up shop at the front.

"No." Mannie shakes his head, but then a look of realization and shock falls across his face. "Oh man. Your dad mentioned the place had changed hands. Maybe they—"

Neither of us waits for him to finish his sentence. Instead, we're up and running, pounding the pavement, dodging pedestrians and rounding the corner of the solarium as fast as our legs will take us.

We get there just in time to see a flash of fur coat and some brunette braids get into a black town car.

"Oh man!" Mannie stamps a foot and throws his camera-free hand into the air. "Was that her?"

I shrug as we watch the car start to back out onto the street. "I don't know. Maybe. Maybe not. Chances are, if we missed it—probably."

Mannie squints at the windows as the car passes us by. "Did I see what I saw? Was she wearing fur? In this heat?"

"I think so."

He lets out a big "ugh."

"I bet it was real fur, too. A kid celebrity, a solarium, and murdered cute animals. That would have made my week."

chapter 20

I hang out and console Mannie until he feels able to run off to another job, then I ride home. When I get there just before 2:00 p.m., I sit on the curb outside my apartment and wait for Jake. At 2:17 p.m. a Hummer, of all things, starts up the street. As soon as I see it, I know it's him. Even before I clock the plates: ML STAR. I kick myself because now I remember seeing them before. I should have remembered and put two and two together when Wendy gave me my banking information.

By the time Jake pulls up to the curb, I am almost doubled over with laughter. "You can't possibly expect me to get into that thing," I say when he swings the door open from inside.

"Hey, think about how I feel. I have to *drive* it!"

I climb in, all the while freaking out about what to do when I get into my seat. Do I kiss him? Not kiss him? Cheek? Lips? I am so not used to this stuff. In the end, when I do settle in, I have to bite my lip to keep from laughing when I realize just how far away Jake is in this gigantic monster vehicle. I couldn't reach him even if I wanted to. "Tell me you don't have a matching Hummer at home," I say to him.

Jake gives me a look. "I have a Mini Cooper at home."

Hmmm. Much better reachability. "Now I'm actually jealous. What color?"

"Red and white."

"Now I think I hate you. That's my dream car. Exact same colors and everything."

"Maybe I could take you for a ride someday to make you hate me less?" Jake says a bit too breezily.

"Maybe. That would be great. Make that definitely."

"Good. You're on. Anyway, um, hi . . ."

Unexpectedly, Jake leans over now and I realize he *is* going to kiss me. Oh. Um. I lean sideways and we end up bumping noses and laughing. Funny, but I don't think Jake is really used to this stuff, either. Which is kind of good. I like that. "Yep, hi to you, too," I say, laughing again.

After we've finished embarrassing ourselves, Jake waits till my belt clicks and then pulls out from the curb.

The GPS directs us to the psychiatric hospital, which is about a forty-minute drive. As we make our way there, we chat easily, like we'd done on the plane. We talk about Ned's treatment, our families, our lives, anything and everything, really.

The whole time, I'm acutely aware of Jake's presence beside me. It's so weird how crazily unstable he makes me feel. One minute I can't stop smiling just because I'm sitting next to him and have to stare out the window and chew on my cheek, the next I'm petrified that he doesn't feel the same way about me as I do about him. In the end, I tell myself now is not the time or place to be thinking about Jake and me. I should be thinking about Ned and what kind of shots I'm going to take of him today. Which I've already stayed up half the night thinking about, but it's more useful going over it one more time than praying that Jake will reach out and touch my knee or something.

It's not until we're almost there that I truly start to get nervous. And I think Jake is, too—suddenly we both become silent and the tension in the car rises palpably. "Think we can pull this off?" I ask with a gulp, my mouth and throat scarily dry.

Jake's eyes remain on the road. "I hope so, Jo. I really hope so. I spent a lot of last night freaking out about what could happen if we don't. I mean, Dad has orchestrated this whole contract, but Ned actually does want it. He wants to get back out there and see his fans again—all over the world. And, let's face it, they've been waiting for him for a while. Ned loves what he does, his phobia just stops him from doing it. It's really cruel. And then there's you, as well. You need to get started on what you love to do."

I'm silent for a moment or two, but then I have to say it: "You're a good person, Jake Hartnett."

Jake shrugs slightly. "It's just . . . the right thing to do is all."

"But most people don't often do the right thing," I tell him. And I'm worried now. Really worried. Our plan is a simple plan that makes sense, and, so far, everything has gone off without a hitch. The people we need to meet with have all agreed to meet, and there have been no problems whatsoever. But now . . . well, now we're actually here, I think, as Jake turns the car into the drive of the hospital and we make our way toward the main building. This is it. Our one big shot to make everything right. For Ned to keep his career and show the public he's not perfect and that anyone, famous or not, might need help. For me to have my new start—to finally do something I'll love instead of detest.

We're here and it's happening.

Good luck to us.

"Nice grounds," Jake says as we pass by the hospital's lush grass, leafy trees, and lots of manicured outside areas for the patients to enjoy.

He's right. It really is lovely. Maybe even nicer than the retreat, which is saying something. And, you've got to admit it's a whole lot warmer—the place certainly has that going for it, too. As Jake pulls in the car a few minutes late, we both look across the parking lot to see everyone is already here waiting for us—Mitchell, the editor I'd called last night, and two other men, who I'm guessing are Ned's cola company contacts.

"Well, Jo . . ." Jake looks across the car at me. He reaches out and grabs my hand, giving it a squeeze.

I take a deep breath. "Here we go!"

We both exit the car and make our way across the parking lot to the group of men. "Sorry we're late," Jake says as we greet them. "It was difficult organizing this on such short notice. I really appreciate you all making it here today."

I introduce Jake to Mitchell and he introduces me to the two men who, as I'd guessed, are reps from the cola company.

To start with, everyone looks slightly awkward, not knowing quite where this is going, how it will work out, or even what they're really doing here. But Jake smoothly directs us all to take a seat at one of the tables underneath a nearby tree and then slowly but surely fills everyone in. He explains how Ned's tired of hiding what's really been going on with him lately and how he's also tired of the media hyping it up into something it's not because they don't know the truth. Jake tells us how part of Ned's recovery involves talking about his feelings rather than suppressing them, and that he'd really like to come out in the open with his phobia and maybe in the process even help other people to admit to, and get help with, their own problems.

Jake makes it all sound so sensible that everyone winds up nodding along with his words and wondering how doing anything else could even have been considered. For a moment or two, when he's outlining how the portraits of Ned will be involved, I get excited and even forget to be nervous. It just all sounds so workable. Finally, he starts to sum up . . .

"What Ned's asking you to do is to work with him." He turns directly to the two reps now. "After all, he's doing really well. There's no reason to think that he won't be able to make public appearances now that he's getting help."

The reps remain silent and my eyes flick from one person to another as I start to wonder if they can hear my stomach. I haven't eaten anything much today because I've been so worried, and this, combined with the stress of finally being here, is making my stomach do a washing machine impersonation. I'm so glad it's Jake doing all the talking, because it's pretty much all I can do to sit here, listen, and wait for my turn to help out, which will come later.

"Look, I understand that you're hesitant to sign him up right now. I would be, too. But think of it this way—you were set to sign him up with all of his problems lurking under the surface. Now that they've come to the fore and he's getting treatment, he's in a more secure place and better able to abide by the terms of a contract than he was before."

More silence.

"And let's not forget that it would be amazing publicity.

Your company will receive a lot more media attention if you move forward with this than if you opt for another star with a cleaner slate."

This gets the reps' attention all right. They both turn and look at Mitchell now, who shrugs slightly. *Come on, Mitchell, I think to myself. Hit it home for them.*

"What can I say?" Mitchell replies, looking at the two reps. "It's true. It's a much better angle than you were originally looking at. You've signed up plenty of stars before, but not one who's actively in a bit of trouble or who needs help. Usually the news we're reporting is that a star's been dropped from his or her contract when something about their past comes to light. But signing up a star with issues? This is big news, there's no denying it."

Phew. I try not to breathe my sigh of relief out loud. *Nice one, Mitch.*

The reps look at each other again. "We might need a few minutes to talk it over," one of them says.

"Of course." Jake nods. "Take your time."

With this, both the reps get up from the table and make their way across the grass and over to the shade of another one of the large trees. Their backs to us, all Jake and I can do is hold our breath and look for meaning in their hand gestures and occasional glances back toward us.

When we're sure they're not listening, Jake turns to me. "How do you think it went?"

"You were brilliant!" I gush, my words tumbling out. It's

only then that I remember that Mitchell is still with us and I sit up a bit, trying to contain myself and all my different emotions.

"This is quite the plan you two have concocted here," Mitchell says, his gaze settling on Jake. "At what point are you going to tell your dad about it?"

Jake groans. "When it's completely, utterly, and totally about to work, he realizes it's the only option left, and we just need his signature on everything."

Mitchell laughs at this. "I'd say that would be just about the right time."

Jake shakes his head. "You know, sometimes I wonder if there's anyone in LA who doesn't know and love my dad. He's such an easy guy to work with."

Mitchell and I say nothing.

"You don't all have to agree with me at once," Jake says with a laugh.

"I wouldn't worry about it too much," I tell Jake. "I'm sure Mitchell's had more than a few encounters with my own dad in his time. Probably demanding more money."

"Um . . . ," Mitchell replies.

"Don't worry." I wave a hand. "Jake and I have already formed a Bad Dads club. Most people would be thrilled their kid wants to go to school and is desperate to study. Mine? He wants me to be a paparazzo when I grow up!"

Mitchell chuckles at this. "Well, I might just join that club. My dad packed me off to military school at fifteen."

"Military school?" Jake and I both ask. I have to admit it feels good to have a distraction going on. I peel my eyes away from the reps and focus in on Mitchell.

He laughs at us. "I know it's hard to believe, but once upon a time, I was a bit of a wild child. At least it was good training to be a newspaper editor. I can hurl a stapler across the room with great accuracy and take down an errant journalist with just two fingers if I have to, thanks to military school."

"I'll keep that in mind," I say, as I notice movement in the distance. The reps look like they're finishing up. Jake and I shoot each other a look, which Mitchell notices.

"You've both got a lot riding on this, don't you?" he asks matter-of-factly.

We nod.

"You know it's something I'm interested in because I have to be," Mitchell continues. "But, for what it's worth, I think you're both doing a good thing here. For Ned, I mean. It's not every day I get to be a part of something like this."

"Thanks, Mitchell," Jake ends up replying for both of us. "It's nice of you to say that." He stands up as the reps approach our bench once more.

There's a pause, in which I have to remind myself to breathe. What will it be? Yes or no?

"Jake," one of the reps says, "I think we can make this happen."

Seriously, I almost jump up on the bench and yell "Yee-ha!"

"But . . ."

Uh-oh. I freeze. I should have known there'd be a "but."

"There'll have to be a few provisos in the contract, of course."

Jake nods, signaling them to go on.

"Ned will need to make those appearances. We'll cut the scheduled ones back a bit, but he has to make at least half of the ones we've already discussed. That's nonnegotiable."

"That sounds more than reasonable," Jake says.

The reps glance at each other. "There's something else, as well."

"Yes?"

"We were wondering if you'd consider coming along. As a kind of stand-in for Ned. You'd need to drop a few pounds of course, but we have to say—the resemblance is remarkable."

Jake glances at me, and in my messy state of angst and joy I stifle a laugh and mouth the words "bacon bits" at him. His mouth twists as he also tries not to laugh. When his attention turns back to the reps, he holds up one hand at their suggestion. "Sorry, but that's not possible. And even if it were possible, it wouldn't be necessary. Ned can do this. I know he can, and I know him better than anyone."

Just as Jake is saying this, we all turn to see Ned himself walking down the grassy slope toward us. We all stand up from the bench. And, as my eyes take Ned in, I can't believe I mistook Jake for him. They're so different. Sure, they might look similar, but really there are more differences than similarities now that I'm looking more closely. Ned walks differently. His expressions are different. His mannerisms are different. And while Jake isn't really *that* much heavier than his brother, there's this leaner, rangy quality to Ned. How could I not have realized this before that moment in the pool? It was my job to notice and I'd brushed away the thoughts that he seemed different. I should have listened to my gut. It had been trying to tell me something all along.

"Hey, bro." Ned walks over to Jake first and gives him a quick hug. "Thanks for organizing this. I really owe you."

"No, you don't." Jake shakes his head. He introduces Ned to Mitchell, but the two reps Ned has already met before.

"And this is Jo. I told you all about her, remember?"

I give Jake a did-you-now? look and he grins.

"She'll be taking some shots today," Jake continues.

One of the cola reps looks a bit confused at this. "Wait. The shots you're talking about. The ones that we'll want to run internationally with the story about what's really been going on with Ned for years. They're going to be taken now? By you?" He turns to me at the last second and shakes his head. "I mean, no offense, sweetheart . . ." He shrugs as he trails off.

Both Jake and Mitchell laugh.

"For a start, Jo is *nobody's* sweetheart," Mitchell begins.

"I've worked with her a lot over the past eighteen months, and she is good. No doubt about it."

"If Jo can't take these shots, no one can," Jake says, backing me up.

The rep still doesn't look convinced. "And we'd be seeing the pictures first?"

"Of course," I say, trying to sound supremely confident. "And you'll love them."

As we talk, Ned tilts his head to one side as he looks at me. "Hang on . . . now that I see you . . . I've heard about you before. You're Zo Jo, right? The paparazzo who runs around getting into places the others can't go?"

My eyes move to Jake's before I answer Ned's question. "Well, I used to be. Not anymore. Now it's just Jo, I guess."

Ned shrugs. "Well, nice to meet you, Just Jo."

I smile as I grab my camera from my backpack.

Just Jo.

My smile gets wider again.

I like it. I like it a lot. Just Jo. I could really get used to a name like that.

chapter 21

After all the wheeling and dealing has been done, it's my turn
to take over for the day. I lead both Jake and Ned across the
grass until we're in a sheltered area, beneath a tree and sur-
rounded from anyone's view by some high shrubs. Then I stop
and give Ned a good once-over. I stand back and really take
him in from head to toe.

"Careful," he ends up telling me, with a grin that matches
Jake's. "I don't want to make my brother jealous."

"That wouldn't be so terrible," I mumble, hoping my
cheeks aren't turning too red and reminding myself to try to
keep things professional. "I need you to get changed," I say to
Ned. "Keep the jeans, but lose the shirt. Just the white T-shirt

you've got on underneath would be great. And ditch the watch, too. Oh, and the shoes and socks." I want this shoot to be pure Ned—no trappings.

In front of Jake and me, Ned starts stripping down. "Always a good look to be losing your clothes on the front lawn of a psychiatric hospital," he says, laughing. Jake and I look at each other for a second and then laugh as well. We've both got to admit it's kind of funny.

As Ned continues getting himself ready, I'm reminded again of something I'd been thinking about last night—that first day at the retreat when I'd opened up the door to room 20 and that light had showered down over Jake. It was an amazing look, and I'm hoping to get some equally dramatic shots today, if I can. It's going to be difficult, though, because the hospital has only allowed us a couple of locations to take photos in—out here on the lawn and in Ned's room—and a set amount of time as well.

"All done," Ned tells me as he hands his watch to Jake, as well as his clothes.

"Since when do I pick up after you?" Jake scoffs.

"Since today," his brother tells him with a grin.

I take a look around me as they bicker. The day is very blue, with only a few patches of clouds. It's not really the look I'm going for. "How about we head inside to your room, first?" I suggest.

"Okay, if you can just put your right arm a bit farther up . . . yep, that's it." I take a few more shots, then check them to see how things are going. "That's good." I nod. "I like it."

We've already spent the past forty minutes or so in Ned's room taking various shots of him—a few sitting very simply, cross-legged, on the plain blond wood desk, a couple staring pensively out the window, and now this sort of constrained shot in which I have him precariously standing on his bed, one arm on the wall and the other on the ceiling. It's a bit Alice in Wonderland—like he's suddenly grown too big for the room and is trying to get out. I like it, though. It's different. And from what Jake told me on the plane, it's a lot like Ned's life has been for the past few years.

I take another series of shots and then check the time. "Um, we'd better get moving. We've only got another half hour or so." Ned has an appointment with his psychiatrist this afternoon that I need to make sure he doesn't miss. I glance around the room quickly, looking for a final opportunity.

"Maybe one last thing," I say to both Ned and Jake. "You can come down now, Ned." I wave him from the bed and grab the simple wooden chair from beneath the desk. I get the two guys to help me pull the bed out and then do some quick furniture rearranging so we end up with an expanse of plain white wall. Then I put the chair in the middle of the space. "Take a seat," I tell Ned. "Just get comfortable."

At first, Ned starts out sitting with one leg crossed on top of the other. Then, after a while, he switches to both feet on the floor. He looks kind of distant, though. I pause for a bit, scrolling through the shots, and as I go, I get an idea that I'd read about in one of my portraiture books.

Ned is really big on keeping connected to his fans online, maybe even more so than other stars because he hasn't been able to meet them in person. I need to show him that what we're doing now is his chance to finally start connecting with them for real and for good—telling them the whole truth about what's been going on in his life.

I look up at Ned from where I'm kneeling on the carpet. "I'm going to take a few more shots, but I want to try something different."

Ned shrugs. "Sure. Fine with me."

"Okay, so this might sound weird, but this time I want you to look straight into the lens and pretend it's like . . . a conduit to your fans. That you can tell them whatever you'd like to tell them through my lens. Does that make any sense?"

Ned nods at me. "Makes perfect sense."

"Great. Let's give it a try."

And, to his credit, Ned does.

It takes me only a couple frames before I know for certain that these are the shots I've been looking for. Because, this time, Ned sits forward with his forearms resting on his thighs and stares straight down my lens just like I asked him to. He doesn't hold back and my gut tells me instantly that I'm getting what I need—what Ned needs. He lets me in, allowing me to see what he's been through and how he's going to get on top of his problems. There's this vulnerability and strength mixed up in his eyes that's highlighted by the simplicity of everything surrounding him—his unadorned white T-shirt, the plain painted wall, the simple chair, his lack of jewelry or watch. And, wow, is he ever handsome. He is one gorgeous guy.

Though maybe not quite as breathtaking as his brother, I think, twisting my mouth to keep from smiling.

As I keep shooting, the room falls silent, and I realize that some moments in my job—my new job—are going to be really special. And this is the first of them. I'm truly honored that Ned's opening up his life and letting me shoot him like this.

I squeeze as many shots into the next five minutes or so as I can. "I think we're done in here," I say, after scrolling through them to check my work. The shots are good—really good. Better than I'd hoped for. I have to take a second to blink back the watery relief, hope, and gratitude that's welling up in my eyes before I glance at Jake and Ned. "Why don't we go back outside now?"

I try taking a few shots of Ned out on the lawn, but I quickly discover they're not right and give up. Instead, I spend our last half hour taking shots of Ned and Jake together.

256

The shots are beautiful—the pair of them joke around and laugh and pretty much behave like a pair of four-year-olds. But it's fun and makes me smile and I can bet it will make other people smile, too.

As I shoot, there's a point at which I see them together, their similar looks and the way they interact with this kind of shorthand, and I get a pang. There's just this sudden, intense stab of pain that hits me and makes me realize I'll never have what they have: a sibling. But while it makes me sad, I don't blame my mom for that. I wish she'd been able to find a better way, some kind of path through which she could move forward without hiding the fact that she was slipping under again, but she couldn't.

For some reason, taking these shots of Jake and Ned gives me a feeling of peace. That, even though I'll never have what they have, I can do this for them. I can capture this fleeting moment in time that will last forever and not just be thrown out with tomorrow's trash. Because I know that they'll keep these photos forever. They'll still be looking at these photos when they're eighty.

It's pretty special to be able to do that for someone.

It's been a long day, and by the time Jake drops me home again, all I can manage to do is heat a frozen meal and flop onto the couch for some TV.

It's the weirdest feeling ever. It's dark and I'm sitting on my butt doing nothing rather than out hitting the pavement, searching for the next great shot. I think about Mannie and what he's doing and send him a quick text.

How're the mean streets of LA?

It takes him a while to respond.

Still there. You thinking about hitting them again?

I send a quick reply.

Not likely. Pulled it off today. Big-time. Better run. Now it's done, going to take your advice and call my dad. Been putting it off.

This time, his reply whizzes back in just seconds.

Nice work, man. Good luck with Papa.

And I'm going to need it, I think to myself as I bring up my dad's number. Before I can stop myself, or think too hard about what I'm doing, I press Dial.

The phone rings only once before it's picked up, which is so my dad. Ever the pap at heart, he's always worried he's going to miss out on something. "One second, love," he says, obviously having read the caller ID. I think he must shove his cell in his pocket or something, because I can hear a kind of rustling. I sit back on the sofa with the TV on mute and wait. "Jo?" he finally answers about thirty seconds later. "You still there?"

"Still here, Dad." I shake my head slightly, but I do it with a smile. I think our phone calls will always run something like this, one of us with a camera in hand, juggling breathing, life, and photography. Not necessarily in that order.

"Oh, good. Sorry about that."

"It's okay." And that's the thing, suddenly it kind of is okay. Maybe the retreat, along with Brad's and Mannie's little parental pep talks, have hit a few things home for me. This is us. Not me. Not him. Us. Talking to Seth had made me think—people deal with things in very different ways. Maybe my dad's "it is what it is" refrain was all he could manage after my mom died, and now it's become a habit for him. There might be bits and pieces of us that I don't like or that drive me up the wall, but at the end of the day, it's who we are. I'm going to have to make the best of what we have. But that doesn't mean I'm going to brush the hard stuff under the rug anymore, either.

"What's up, Jojo?"

"Well . . ." I'm suddenly nervous and have to stop to take a deep breath. "I'm just calling to say I'm done. I'm getting out."

"So you finished up that job for Melissa?"

"Kind of."

"Kind of?" My dad is smarter than that.

I take the next few minutes to flesh out my story, including how I brought Mitchell in at the last minute and my portraits of Ned. There's a long silence when I'm done.

"Knew you were a chip off the old block. That's some serious wheeling and dealing, Jo. Good for you, kid."

I laugh at this. There're probably not many dads out there who'd actually congratulate you on being a lying, cheating, two-timing double agent. But it looks like one of those dads is mine.

Luckily.

"Thanks, Dad," I say. And then I remember Mannie. "Oh, and you owe me sixty thousand dollars."

Now it's my dad who laughs. "You really are my daughter! Straight to the invoice, eh?"

I decide to cut him a break. "Well, you don't really owe me that much. I've done the math, and I probably only need around fifty grand. Mitchell's money covered most of what I gave back to Matthew Hartnett, but not all of it."

Silence on the other end of the line.

"I know it's a lot," I add. "But then I can get out. For good. Please, Dad, I really need to. Before the business swallows me alive." My voice sounds pathetically desperate.

"So, you're offering your old man a discount? That's sweet."

"I—" I start, but my dad cuts in.

"Love, you should have told me if you hated it that much. I don't want you to be miserable every day of your life. I knew you weren't keen, but I didn't know it was that bad."

He didn't? I think of Mannie now. Maybe he was right. Maybe I've only been seeing things from my point of view? I open my mouth to say something, but my dad beats me to it.

"Ah, well, there goes the dream that my daughter, the paparazzo, would follow in my footsteps. *Poof!* Sweetheart, it'll be in your account tomorrow. Things are going well enough here to cover it. And I guess the old heart will recover from the pain. *I'm* going to ask for something else, though."

My heart skips a beat when I hear this. There's a catch? "What's that?"

"A trip over here, of course. When are you coming already?"

"To Tokyo, you mean?"

"Yes, to Tokyo. You've got another two weeks or so before school starts, right? I was going to come home for a few days, but why don't you come here?"

Huh. That's funny. I didn't know he wanted me to come over at all. I pause for a second before replying. "Well," I finally say, "that'd be . . . nice. And I guess I'm pretty free as far as time goes, being unemployed and all . . ."

Epilogue

Jake did exactly what he said he was going to do and brought his father in on the plan at the very last second. When Matthew Hartnett finally found out what had been going on behind his back, he was not a happy man . . .

Until he realized that, this time, he'd actually be gaining more publicity by using the truth than by his usual deceptive means. Then Jake became the best son in the world.

Right after Ned, of course.

Not that Jake cared. He was just happy that Ned was doing better every day, had already made a handful of small public appearances that had gone amazingly well, and that, finally, they could both put that horrible moment from their past behind them.

Mitchell ended up paying me around half the money that Melissa (or should I say ML Entertainment?) had promised to pay me. Between my dad's generosity and rearranging my study plans a bit, I managed to not have to resort to selling baked potatoes.

Melissa actually got laid off from her job not long after Ned signed his cola contract. At first I was kind of hopeful that she'd find it hard to get a job and have a lot of time to sit around her apartment and realize the error of her ways, but sadly, this didn't happen. Not even close. Instead, she was snapped up and became editor of one of the sleaziest tabloids out there, which was probably always her dream job, anyway.

That's LA for you.

I took my dad up on the offer of the trip to Tokyo. We had an amazing time together. I stayed for nine days and he showed me Tokyo; then we took the bullet train down to Hiroshima and Kyoto. Japan was a photographer's dream. I went nuts and took about a million photos a day. Especially in Kyoto. Kyoto, with its huge number of temples and shrines, was like going back in time.

I think I saw more of Japan through my lens than I did with my actual eyes. I even got to see the house where my mom grew up, where she went to school, and the area that would have been the most familiar place on earth to her— Shibamata, a neighborhood on the edge of Tokyo. I may not have been lucky enough to get to know my mom, but that trip made me feel a little like I did. Dad shared a lot of things about her that I hadn't known because I don't think he'd been brave enough to tell me and I hadn't been brave enough to ask.

While I was away, Mitchell ran the story about Ned. The shots looked even better than I expected (I'm as modest as my dad, too). And the response was huge. Huger than huge, actually. Both Ned and Jake were thrilled with all the support Ned got for finally coming clean. Even Matthew Hartnett was pleased, which is saying something for him. A number of magazines and even a few stars got in contact with me through Dad's website, and I have leads for a couple of jobs.

So, what's next? Well, school, of course (Ms. Forman is making sure of that). I'm hanging out for winter break, though, because Dad found this amazing weeklong portraiture course in NYC, which means I'll get to hang out with Jake, like old times at the retreat.

Speaking of the retreat, I sent an e-mail to Brad a few days ago, thanking him for the time he spent with me and the advice he gave me. In a roundabout, as few details as possible, kind of way, I managed to explain what had gone on. Knowing Brad, I'm sure he's more than smart enough to fill in the blanks.

Since leaving the retreat I've spoken to Katrina twice, and IM'd a good couple of times, too. She's loving being back at home with her sisters and squabbling over the bathroom. She's decided to give up her ballet training and concentrate on her Pilates, with just the occasional ballet class on the side. She even hopes to open up her own Pilates studio after college.

I've caught up with Seth a few times online, too. He has this blog he's been writing that makes me laugh. It's called *Crazy on the Inside.* He's talking about writing a book about his experiences, and I think he could do it, too.

Oddly, I've been seeing more of Mannie than I used to when we were working. I've been giving him heaps of tips on using my equipment, and sometimes, just for fun, I'll go out to work with him in the evening to keep him company (okay, and to tie some of the other paps' shoelaces together so he gets better shots).

So, that's it for me. A clean start. A new life.

But first I have a promise to keep. Before I left LA, someone asked if they could sit for me and I couldn't say no. A certain someone named . . .

Ned Hartnett.

Yes, again. No great surprise there, but hey, I'm just starting out. And in this game, you've got to use the contacts you have. He'll be in NYC at the same time I'm going to be there for my course.

Jake's even promised to act as my assistant for Ned's second shoot. I told him I can't afford one yet, but he said that's fine.

For me, he's happy to take payment in bacon bits.

And kisses on demand.

Acknowledgments

I'd like to thank my amazing agent, Sara Megibow, for spotting the story beneath the rubble, and my editor, Stacy Cantor Abrams, for being willing to take it on and polish it up.

Also, the ever-supportive group of writers at teenlitauthors.

My husband and kids. This book would have been written a lot faster if it weren't for them, but life would not have been nearly as interesting!

And I couldn't forget our assortment of Devon Rex cats who danced on the keyboard and slept on my lap at various points during the writing process.